THE LIES WE tell

For my hubby and mom, who both told me to KEEP WRITING.

becca

"So, you're going to just be a big, fat liar?"

"No, I am going to be a big, fat 'don't ask, don't tell' advocate," I sang as I shoved more clothes into my suitcase.

My best friend, Ali, crossed her arms, clearly annoyed with how I was glossing over her concerns. "That isn't the context the phrase was founded on."

"Well, that phrase is my new motto, so it doesn't matter."

"I just think you're overreacting, Becs. Be proud of who you are!"

"I am proud. I just want to separate myself from my brother. I don't want just to be Cam Nichols' sister my entire life."

Ali sighed, knowing she would lose that battle again. No matter how crazy she thought I was, she had no idea what it was like being me. My entire adult life, people had handed me whatever I wanted because of who my brother was—the star at everything. Just once, I wanted to earn something myself, without his influence.

Because I knew I could do it.

"It's going to be hard, considering you will be working for the

Kings. Kace will be there every day. He knows who you are. How will you avoid the unavoidable?"

"Yeah," I sighed, squinting and pointing at Ali. "I need to have a talk with that boyfriend of yours. He needs to avoid me like the plague and keep out of my business."

Ali was the only person I'd told about my last-minute job offer working with the Atlanta Kings, our city's professional baseball team. It was a low-paying, internship in Florida, and only during spring training, but it held a lot of promise for a long-term position.

Since graduating with my Sports Medicine degree, I had worked for local high schools and their athletic departments. There was less pressure than the college and pro levels, and even though I knew I was good at what I did, I was afraid of being accepted just because of who my brother was.

Cam was the quarterback of the Atlanta Jets, the professional football team. He always assured me that I could use his name to get a job, then prove my worth when I got there. He thought I was crazy not to. But almost everyone on the team knew who I was, and I didn't want to be treated like Cam Nichols' sister.

When the opportunity to join the Kings fell into my lap, I realized most of them didn't know who I was, and I would be able to prove myself on my own. There was just the small matter of Kace Jackson, my brother's best friend and Ali's other boyfriend. She was also dating Cam, which made the circle of confusion start small.

"You know, your brother and Kace played those hidden identity games with me. Does this run in the family or something?" Ali had one eyebrow hitched, questioning me.

Six months or so ago, Cam and Kace played a game of *Guess Who* with Ali and lied through their teeth about who they were. Their lie may, or may not, have played a role in Ali being found by her abusive ex.

"This is different," I reasoned. "I'm not trying to attract a man into my life by hiding who I am. I'm trying to prove who I can be in this city without the glitter surrounding anyone with the last name Nichols." Stuffing more clothes into my bag, I was anxious and ready, even if I didn't leave for two more days when pitchers and catchers were due to report.

"I guess," Ali sighed once again. "So, they just never questioned your last name being Nichols?"

"Um," I cringed a little before answering. "I told my boss my name was Becca Nichols. I just didn't give him the chance to connect the dots. I told him I was from the Midwest and new to town, so there was no connection to Cam. And when I get into the locker room, no one will have to know my last name. They won't ask, and I won't tell."

Even though I sounded like an idiot, I waved my hands around as if I had just presented her with gold. Until it all blew up in my face, I was going with lies and omissions when necessary.

Ali muttered, "Liar," under her breath as her phone started to ring. As if I were a child, I stuck my tongue out at her while she lifted her phone to answer it.

"Hello?"... "I'm at your sister's apartment watching her pack."..." Oh no, I'm going to let her tell you herself."..." It's not bad, Cam, relax. But grab Kace and meet us at my place in a bit. Becca has a fun story to tell Kace before he leaves for spring training." Ali was eyeing me with a glint of amusement, ready to see their reactions to my plan.

Waving her off, I tried acting like I didn't care. But I did. Kace was a wildcard. My spring job would be a bust if he didn't agree to act like he didn't know me. It wasn't just me that had to lie, Kace had to as well. Seriously though, why should he even care? It wasn't like he and I were best friends. He was simply best friends with my brother, and dating my best friend—we barely knew each other.

Now I was lying to myself.

Kace was more like a second brother—one I used to dream about doing dirty things with. Despite being younger than me by a year, he and Cam had looked after me, and my two older sisters, since they were in elementary school. They were always bigger and tougher than everyone else, and it was a gift they took advantage of.

They were nine when they punched my first bully.

They were eleven when they punched my first crush.

They were twelve when I started crushing on Kace.

They were fourteen when I hated both of them and wished them dead.

They were sixteen when I realized they were both destined to be professional athletes.

You get the picture. It goes without saying that Cam had always been in my life; he was my brother. But Kace had been too. So, how was I going to convince him to pretend he didn't know me?

"Hey, Becs," Ali clapped, bringing me back to the real world. "We're going to my place at seven."

"Yeah, so I heard."

As well as knowing Kace Jackson my whole life, I also saw him regularly. Once Ali and I connected and became friends, the reasons for us to be around each other doubled. They had adopted me as their fourth wheel.

"Please tell me you brought pizza!" I begged as Cam walked into the door holding a small bag of food with Kace right behind him.

"Pizza?" Cam looked down at the bag that was clearly not a 16-inch square full of cheesy goodness. "I got Thai."

"Eh, that'll work," I shrugged, playing the petulant sister even though we all knew I loved Thai. Giving my brother shit was how I coped with being their awkward fourth wheel.

"So, Ali said you're packing. Where ya going?" Cam wasted no time, wanting to know my plans before he even unpacked the food.

"What, I don't get to eat first?"

"Is it that big of a deal, that you need food to tell us about your travels?" Cam waved a hoity hand in the air. He probably thought I was headed abroad to backpack the wineries in Italy. His smug face made me eager to tell him I was headed to his worst brotherly nightmare.

"Here's a clue. I'm headed where Kace is headed."

Kace looked over at me, confused. "Florida?"

"Yesss. But not just anywhere in Florida," I teased.

"Miami Beach?" Cam shrugged. "You love the beach."

"Noooo, geez. I'm an athletic trainer. Helloooo."

It took another minute, but I laughed the second I realized Cam had caught on and his face paled. "You got a job with a baseball team?"

"Not just any team, the Kings!"

Cam stopped unpacking the food and looked at me with more relief than I was expecting. *Why did he look relieved?* He should have been telling me how much he hated that I wouldn't just work for the Jets, and all that same stuff he always told me.

"That's a great job opportunity, Becs. Congrats!"

"I thought you'd hate the idea of me going the baseball route and not taking you up on a recommendation." My eyes were locked on his, curiosity making me unable to eat.

"Oh, this works out just as well," he shrugged, then smirked at me. "Kace will be there."

Ali started laughing, already knowing what Cam was thinking. Cam and Kace looked at each other and suppressed their laugh, also knowing something I clearly didn't.

"What does that matter?"

"Kace will keep just as close of an eye on you as I would, so Jets or Kings. Either works out well."

"No," I snapped quickly. "Kace isn't going to 'brother' me."

"Yes I am," Kace responded around a mouth full of food. "You know we've always watched out for you. That isn't changing any time soon."

"Kace," I whined, "I need you to act like you don't know me. Not overprotect me."

"What? Why?"

"Because, if you don't, then everyone will know I'm Cam's sister. The whole world knows how close you two are, and I seriously don't want anyone making that connection."

"Why?" Cam repeated Kace, wanting me to keep explaining myself.

"Because," I stressed, "I got this job on my own merit, and I want to keep it on my own merit. At the end of spring training, these teams take their interns, and potentially hire them for the full season. I don't want that job because of who I know."

"So you want me to lie?" Kace asked.

"By omission," I explained. "Don't acknowledge me, and I won't acknowledge you."

"How will that work? They usually assign the interns into sections based on position. What if you get infielders? I'm a shortstop, and you would be all up in my business. It's going to be hard to pretend you're not like a sister to me when you have to massage my thighs."

For fuck's sake.

"I've already been assigned to catchers. I have to be there in two days when catchers and pitchers report."

Kace huffed, probably thinking I was an idiot for caring about this as much as I did, but I didn't care. He was once a liar about who he was, so I was ready to pounce with the hypocrite card if he didn't agree to pretend he didn't know me.

"Okay, Becs. I will ignore the shit out of you," Kace agreed. "But I *will* be keeping an eye on you. If anybody gets out of line, I will punch their face in and send you home."

"You can punch them all you want, but I'm not going home just because you say so. This is an incredible chance for me to work at a pro-level. I'm going to make it through these next six weeks and prove I can hack it." Crossing my arms, I stared down l Kace and my brother until I was sure they were on board.

"What about when Ali and I come down to spend time with Kace and watch some games? You gonna ignore us, too?" Cam finally asked.

Looking at him like he lost his damn mind, I laughed humorlessly. "Of course, I will. You're the main reason I'm lying in the first place."

chase

I was only thirty-three years old, but my knees were shot. I could barely stand out of bed without pain in the mornings. Being a baseball catcher since high school wasn't exactly good on the knees.

All the squatting.

Up and down.

Up and down.

For years.

Everyday.

Usually, I kept myself in check during the offseason, but it got harder every year. Over spring training, I had to hope that I could get back into full form. Especially since it was a contract year for me. If the team caught a whiff of the pain I was in, there was a chance I could be replaced with the new, and young, draftees that were invited to spring training.

Not to mention that would be the cheaper option for the team, as well. I was paid like the veteran I was, which was a lot more than the young guys with fresh knees. I couldn't let them sniff out any weakness in my game. In fact, I had to be better than I ever was if I wanted the contract the team would owe me.

Spread out on the floor, I attempted to stretch before I even had to leave the hotel for the first day. It was my home away from home, where the entire team took over—players, management, trainers, staff, owners, scouts, etc.

Most of the guys invited their wives and kids to stay as well. But not me. It wasn't that I didn't want to invite my wife and kids, it's just that I didn't have any. Which worked out well for me. With plans on five more years of baseball before I was ready to call it quits, it was easier not having to worry about the responsibility of a family.

One day I wanted kids. Someone to teach the game to. Just not right then. My only focus was getting my knees to cooperate.

When stretches were done, I hopped in the shower hoping the warm water would soak into my bones and help me rid myself of the limp I was dealing with. Then I got dressed in athletic shorts and a t-shirt and walked into the hall at the same time the door across from me opened.

"Yo, Cap!" I called out to our team captain, Kace Jackson, as he shut his door.

"Hey, Turner," he mumbled, lacking the enthusiasm he usually had.

"Whoa, what's up? Why are you here already? Don't you guys report in a week?" Only the pitchers and the catchers were supposed to be there, and Kace was an infielder. He should have been soaking in one more week of freedom.

"Yeah," he sighed as we started walking toward the elevator. "I just needed to go ahead and get here. Since last season ended the way it did, I felt like I should come early."

No matter how the previous season ended, and for him, it was a doozy, he didn't have to be there. He may have been six years younger than me, but he wore the captain's patch for a reason—because he fucking deserved it.

So his reasoning felt like somewhat of a lie.

"Trouble in paradise?"

Kace and my buddy, Cam Nichols, had been sharing a girl-friend since the season ended last year, and I felt that was bound to go south eventually. They may have been close, but could they really both date the same girl and not be affected?

"Not at all," Kace scoffed, as if I was way off base. At least that time he sounded believable.

Deciding to let it go, I concluded he was just there to show the team how dedicated he was despite missing the playoffs with us the year before. "Well, glad you're here, Cap."

As we rode the elevator down to the lobby, we switched gears and talked about the offseason. I filled him in on my offseason travels, which were just a bunch of lies, and he updated me on his vacation with Cam and their girl after Cam's football season ended.

Chit chat.

That was what all it was. Guys hated chit chat, but it was what we did when we were putting in the effort to distract one another. For me, it was to distract Kace from my limp. There was no telling why Kace was humoring me, though.

When the elevator doors opened, I stepped out into the lobby and headed toward the shuttle that would take us to the stadium. But I was only five steps out when I stopped dead in my tracks and a sudden shiver ran down my spine. It took me a minute, but I shook off the sensation, and chalked it up to being the pain in my knee traveling up to tell my brain to sit the fuck down.

'Coming?" Kace waited for me to get my shit together, so I resumed walking next to him for another few more steps. Something pulled my gaze to the right, though, and I stopped again.

Only that time, I knew exactly what had gotten into me.

The most gorgeous woman I had ever seen stood by the hostess in the hotel restaurant. Dark blonde hair, tanned skin, and emerald eyes. She had tight jeans that hugged just right, and a t-shirt that hung off one shoulder. Fuck, I was hypnotized, having never felt such an immediate attraction to a woman.

It was safe to assume she was staying at the hotel, but who knew for how much longer? My hope was for at least for one more night because I had plans for that body that I needed to see through—knees be damned.

Walking away from Kace, I made my way toward where she was standing. It may have been my only chance to get her phone number and I needed it before I could think about working out that day. Hell, I'd settle for just her name, or her Facebook, an email address, her Twitter handle, geographical coordinates.

Something.

Unfortunately, I didn't make it far before Kace caught up and stopped me, grabbing me by the shoulder and turning me back around.

"What the fuck, Cap?"

"Not her," Kace growled.

"Why the fuck not?" My words were harsh and clipped, making him flinch and remove his hands from my shoulders.

"Just trust me."

"Cap, I trust you with the game-winning play and I trust you at the plate in the bottom of the ninth with two outs. But I don't think I can trust you with her. Besides, I'm not gonna ask her to marry me, just get her in my bed tonight." Why the fuck was I explaining myself to him? He may have been the captain of the team, but he wasn't in charge of my life.

"Just trust me." His voice got lower and lethal, making me take a second look at his face to see what the hell his problem was. For some reason, we were having a standoff over a stranger, and I wanted to know why.

Kace didn't explain, but his vehemence made me think twice.

For a minute.

When I thought about it a third time, though, I remembered the legs on that woman and started toward her again, giving Kace a middle finger as I walked away.

Unfortunately, it only took me a second to realize that she

had disappeared in the time I spent looking at Kace. She was gone, along with any chances I had of sliding between her legs later on.

Fucking Kace.

Looking back at him, I realized he was also gone. Only catching the sight of his back as he exited the hotel to board the team shuttle. Defeated, I followed along.

There would be more women walking through the hotel in the coming weeks. Honestly, they were everywhere in the Sunshine State. Plus, being who I was meant never being at a loss for women at my feet.

But being cockblocked by Kace somehow made me want *that* woman even more.

becca

THERE WASN'T MUCH TO HATE ABOUT FLORIDA. PALM TREES AND sunshine were everywhere. And, it was February and warm. The ocean was only a few miles in one direction, and Disney World was just up the road the other way. It really was the happiest place on earth.

Until I saw Kace come out of the damn elevator that morning.

He and Cam agreed that Kace would go early to spring training and keep an eye on me, which pissed me off. When were they going to learn that I was a grown woman and didn't need them to babysit me?

Kace had been walking with Chase Turner, the veteran catcher with the Kings. Luckily, I saw them when Chase's back was to me, shot Kace an evil glare for even being there, and then ran. I didn't even get to sit down and eat breakfast, or change into my work clothes.

Kace may have promised to pretend like he didn't know me, but I didn't want to face him before I even got to the field. I needed more time to steel my face for the lies I was about to tell.

Instead of taking the team shuttle, I ordered an Uber to the stadium. The silence gave me time to prepare myself. Breathe. And hope Kace held up his end of the bargain.

He wouldn't blow my secret because Ali would kill him, right?

When I reached the double doors leading to the locker room and offices, I returned to being the Becca I wanted to be while I was there. Determined and hardheaded. Smart and ambitious.

After changing into my team-issued khakis and polo shirt, I made my way to the common areas to introduce myself to my fellow interns. Several of the players had walked through while we stood there, and I politely smiled and nodded. Except for Kace, I just ignored him, but to his credit, he didn't look my way, either.

But Chase Turner did. He eyed me like he knew all my secrets. Like Kace had spent their entire elevator and shuttle ride telling him all the fun details about me. He was frozen, causing a few others to have to walk around him. He continued to stare at me until I broke the connection by returning to face my new fellow interns.

He knew. Shit, did he know? I wouldn't be able to think straight until I broke my own rules and talked to Kace to see what Chase knew.

Until that morning, I had almost forgotten about Chase. He was friends with my brother, but they didn't go out of their way to hang out. Maybe it came up, though, that Cam had a sister who was into sports medicine. Sometimes Cam and I look alike, so he may have just put two and two together.

"So, are we supposed to be friends or enemies?" One of the other interns broke me from momentarily overthinking as he laughed at his own question. His name was Jason, maybe.

"I think some good-natured competition is good for us," another one said. *Joey?*

"Yeah, but I need this job at the end of spring training, so go ahead and make sure you all stay out of my way," the third one joked. *Mark?*

I knew I had the names right, but I couldn't remember who was which because I hadn't been paying enough attention.

"What about you?" The one I think was named Jason was looking at me. "Seems like you're the only girl. Think you can handle this? Or maybe they will just give you a pass for being a chick?"

"Well, technically," I scrunched my nose at what he was implying and thought about what I should say. "I'm not a girl. I'm a woman. A very smart woman. So I think I can handle just about anything." I didn't mean to sound like a bitch, but I didn't want them undermining me either. Thinking I got a pass because I was a woman would be worse than thinking I got there because of who my brother was.

They stayed silent, though. Probably determining whether I was indeed a bitch and if they wanted to deal with that. Either way, I would be fine. I didn't need to make friends. Friends had a way of figuring shit out.

"Okay, okay, listen up." The head athletic trainer, Gary, was walking up, joining our group. "You four have been hired for the spring only. We have an influx of players here trying to make the team, which means we need all the hands we can get. You all have been briefed on how this works when you were hired. Show us you can cut it around here, and you could become a junior trainee with the team in Atlanta. Or maybe not. That is up to you."

He gestured for us to follow and led us down a hallway to two sets of double doors. "Those doors to the right are locker room doors. You have access to the locker room should you need it. However," he pointed to the other set of doors, "those doors lead to the training room and training equipment. That is where we will spend most of our time. The players come to us because that is where we are equipped to handle their aches and pains."

Getting increasingly excited as we entered the training room, I tried to take in everything around me as quickly as possible.

The space was so much more impressive than high school-level equipment. There were a dozen tables lined up in the middle of the room. Around the sides of the room were cabinets and counters full of medical supplies. Through a glass wall on the side, I could see a room of training equipment and exercise machines.

"Uh, Becca, right?" Gary asked me once we were in a semi-circle again.

"Yes, sir."

"You are with the catchers. There are four of them reporting to spring training. You're also the only female on staff that has access to the locker room. Use that power wisely. Don't screw up. No ogling any players, it's inappropriate. And no relationships will be allowed. It's too messy, and we don't do that here."

I got where he was coming from, but to be singled out—again—because of my gender was getting old, fast.

"I assure you I'm a professional, Gary. And I have no interest in men." Whoa, where did that lie come from? I meant to say *these* men. "But don't forget to warn these ladies as well," I pointed to my three male counterparts. "I don't trust the way they ogled the players when they walked in."

Joey—or Jason—rolled his eyes at me. "Okay, okay. No more, 'Becca is a woman' comments."

I actually laughed, which lightened the mood.

"Alright, Becca, go introduce yourself to the catchers, let them know who you are, and what they need to come to you for." Gary handed me a clipboard with a list of names, jersey numbers, and a short introduction of each player's past medical issues. "All the players come in and get a baseline set up, so make sure you start with physicals, and turn those into me by the end of the week. Anything over your head. you carry the issues up the ranks. I'm going to get these *ladies*," he thumbed toward the other interns, "started on the pitchers and any other early reporting players."

Smiling, I enjoyed how well Gary had responded to me, along with the other guys.

After telling everyone to have a good day, I headed for the locker room, and as I pushed the double doors open, I started shaking with excitement. No matter who my brother was, or how well I knew Kace, I was a huge fan of the Atlanta Kings. I always had been. They were my hometown team, after all. So, walking into their space for the first time was exhilarating.

Standing still for a minute, I looked around and took in my surroundings. There were lockers lining both walls, and down the middle were tables, leather couches, and recliners. Everything was intricately detailed and no expense had been spared. A few players were scattered at the lockers and talking amongst themselves so no one had noticed me yet.

Or so I thought.

Chase was sitting at his locker, elbows on his knees, and his head tilted. His eyes were on me again, like he knew something about me. Something he didn't like. Which reminded me I needed to talk to Kace.

Since Chase was the team's number one catcher, I knew I would be working with him eventually. But I mentally moved him to last on my introductions list, buying me some time before I had to face him and find out what his deal was.

It didn't take as long to chat with the other catchers as I had hoped, and before I knew it, the only person left was Chase.

As I headed his way, Kace cut across the locker room with his phone to his ear and a goofy smile on his face. It was a good chance to finally talk to him, but there were still too many people around. Including Chase, who had been watching me the whole time.

The phone to Kace's ear gave me an idea, though. I couldn't call him myself, but I bet he was talking to Ali and she could be our go-between.

Are you on the phone with Kace?

Yes… why?

Can you tell him to meet me in the training room,
in the closet in the back?

You want me to tell my boyfriend to meet you in
a closet?

You know I can't talk to him out in the open. And
I need to ask him a question.

Glancing up at Kace, I saw he was still talking to Ali, and hoped she was relaying my message. When he looked at me back and laughed, I knew she had told him what I needed.

He said to just ask him now. You're twenty feet
away from him.

Is he insane?? I'm not talking to him here with
everyone around.

No, like, ask me, and I will ask him.

Oh my God.

I saw him and Chase Tuner in the lobby this
morning, and now Chase keeps looking at me
like I killed his dog. Did he tell Chase my secret?
Or does Chase know somehow?

I waited a few minutes, acting like I was working and discussing *'work things'* with someone on my phone. Then I heard Kace laugh out loud across the room, and I wanted to punch his throat.

He better not be laughing at me.

Haha. He is. But he said he didn't tell him. Chase
noticed you, and he warned Chase to back off,
that's all.

That practically screamed, *"She's my best friend's sister and I promised to kill on his behalf."*

Well, Chase keeps giving me the hate-eye.

Kace said Chase doesn't know who you are, so he must hate you for a different reason.

Was he serious right now? Did he not realize how nervous I was?

Great. Thanks. I have to go meet him now. Maybe he will tell me why he hates me.

Have fun. I will send you Kace's new number in case you need him for anything else.

No, don't do that. If I need him, I will text you. It's easier to lie when he's not in my contacts.

As you wish. Be safe. Have fun.

Sliding my phone back into my pocket, I scanned the room for Chase again. He was no longer looking at me, but was still sitting at his locker, doing something to his catcher's mitt.

As I approached, he glanced up and I waved. "Hi. I'm Becca, the training intern assigned to catchers for the spring."

For professional reasons, I reached my hand out for him to shake, but inside, I was a freaking out. He took a minute, but then he stood to his full height and reached out, slowly taking my hand.

Chase was taller than I thought he was, and definitely broader. Muscles were everywhere I could see, and probably everywhere I couldn't. But my eyes were transfixed on our hands, staring at them as if that simple handshake confused me.

I was beguiled by his touch. The unexpected sensation was almost more than I could handle. His hand was so warm, and with his arms so large and powerful, they made me want to envelope myself in them—a very unwelcome feeling.

"Hi," he said solemnly, then dropped my hand quickly, making me wonder if he had felt the energy run through him, as well.

"Is there anything you need from me before you head out there?" I asked.

His eyes squinted, and he looked off into the area around us, focusing on nothing in particular. "Nope. Fit as a fiddle."

It felt forced—a small fib. But I made a note to keep an eye on him and report what I saw, regardless.

"Well, okay then, Chase Turner," I made a show of checking his name off my list. "Find me if you need me. I will be with Manny Fernandez in the training room."

His jaw ticked slightly in annoyance, but I didn't understand why. His short nod was his only response before he walked off.

With one interaction, I felt like I had run ten miles, exhausted, and completely out of breath. I ran a hand over my head, pushing the stray hairs from my ponytail off my face as my phone buzzed in my pocket.

> Kace said that looked brutal.

I glanced up at Kace, who was buried in his locker, not looking my way, but still on the phone with Ali. I didn't bother responding. He was right. It was brutal. I just wish I understood why.

chase

Seeing the sexy woman from the hotel standing in the gateway of the stadium was by far the most unexpected high, and crushing low I had ever experienced in one flash. She was there, but she was fucking working.

Working.

A trainer. An intern, no less.

That was a worst-case scenario because I had to be around her and couldn't even touch her. It pissed me off for a reason I wasn't even sure I could explain.

And how did Kace know? Why didn't he just say as much?

Trust me, he had said.

I shrugged that off and focused on Becca as she walked from the locker room following our introduction. Something was making me uncomfortable, and I escaped by walking to the bulletin board on the wall like it was vital to my career that I read all the information posted for incoming rookies.

It wasn't.

She seemed rattled to meet me, though. It may have been because I was glaring at her with an annoyed *'what the fuck'* look. But I couldn't help it. It wasn't fair that I wanted her and couldn't have her. Interoffice relationships were a huge no-no, and despite working on a field, and in a locker room, it was essentially just that—our office–and we all worked there.

Taking a peek at Kace, I noticed he was still on the phone. Then I looked at a table and saw a few young pitchers sharing their curveball secrets. Over by the door leading to the field, the one I should have been headed through to get my stretching in, were a couple of young catchers I would be mentoring throughout the spring.

And finally, I looked at my hand. The one I touched Becca with. It was shaking, and felt like it was on fire, so I shook it out, stretched my fingers, and shook it again.

"One more minute, Chase, that is all you get," I whispered to myself. It was time to forget my knee pain, the new trainer, Kace being weird, and the offseason.

Deep breath.

It was time to lie through my teeth.

"So, you spent the offseason fucking your way through Greece?" Ethan asked.

Even being as young as he was, Ethan Jones was our number-one pitcher. Every spring, he and I started the season together–bonding, throwing the ball around, and bullshitting. It got us reacquainted with each other's styles, and made our catcher/pitcher combination more sound.

"Pretty much," I shrugged, then threw the ball at him.

Truthfully, I didn't fuck my way through Greece. I visited Greece for a week, and then sat with my drunk father in my apartment, pretending everything was okay, just so I could make it through the holidays. But I'd already established that I was a liar, and the last thing I wanted was someone giving me shit for my dad's issues. No off-field distractions were going to seep through my facade.

The last ten years of my life as a pro player had been spent living it up. The king of the catchers in Major League Baseball. But in a matter of months, things had changed so drastically. My dad deciding to be an alcoholic was just the tip of the iceberg. Babysitting him had kept me off the field all off-season, and undoubtedly the reason I was struggling with my knees. Just thinking about my knees made me grimace as Ethan and I continued to toss the ball back and forth.

"You okay? Need me to call the trainer?" Ethan paused his throw, noticing my change.

"Fuck off. I'm fine. You know I'm always good."

After a few more warm-up tosses, I squatted to catch Ethan's pitches. We worked on calls, signs, and techniques. Powering through my personal problems was easier when I was out on the field, in my element.

As the day went on, a few other starting pitchers joined our bullpen session, and we worked on issues in their throws. Time flew by, and before I knew it, the sun was setting, making us call it a day.

Approaching the dugout to enter the locker room, I spotted Becca leaning on the rails. Her arms were crossed, and she was staring at me intently, seemingly in deep thought. I imagined her taking mental notes on everything she saw, which made me slow my pace.

When the others passed me and left, she still stood there, staring. Getting closer to her, I wanted to ask her what the hell her problem was, but I couldn't risk losing the control I had regained on the field that day. So, I kept walking past her until she spoke first.

"You're hurting," she muttered quietly.

The fuck?

I paused for a moment, not sure what to say, or do. How could she know I was hurting? Other than that brief moment of concern from Ethan, the guys I'd spent years working with didn't catch on. So how could she?

Instead of responding at all, I continued walking down the hallway toward the locker room. She stayed put, not following me, and making me more unnerved.

Maybe I should have denied it. But I didn't.

Maybe I didn't want to lie to her.

Or maybe I was pissed she saw through me so easily.

becca

THE FIRST WEEK WENT BY FAST. I STAYED BUSY, AND THE RUSH from working with big leaguers made the days seem short. I mostly did physical therapy with the catchers, stretching them out before practice, and patching them up afterward.

I was also able to get baseline physicals done on everyone.

Almost everyone.

Chase never came to see me. He never seemed to need anything. When I asked the other interns if they had seen him, they told me they hadn't seen him either.

Impossible.

Being an athlete required taking care of their bodies as thoroughly as they could. In Chase's brief history report, he consistently sought before and after care for muscles and joints.

His change in routine didn't go unnoticed by just me, either. Gary had asked me what procedures Chase had been given, and I had no answer.

"Get him in the shop, give him that check-up. Tell him we need a new baseline," Gary demanded.

Sure, Gary, that sounds super easy.

The rest of the team was supposed to be getting to spring

training the next day, and games started the day after that. So, there was no time left to let Chase make his own decisions.

Easing into the locker room, I quietly looked around for Chase. He was playing cards at a table with a few pitchers and Kace.

Great. Not only did I have to get Chase's attention, but I also had to do it with witnesses.

"Hey, Chase?" I called from the door, wanting to avoid approaching their table.

Kace and the other guys looked at me with normal, curious expressions. Chase, on the other hand, raised his eyebrows, looking surprised that I dared to bother him.

"I need you in the training room," I added.

"I'm good," he sighed, then turned back to his game. His brush off was expected, but I still wasn't sure where to go from there. I had really hoped he'd say, *"Okay,"* and follow me.

Why was he making this hard?

"Actually, Turner, you don't understand." I thought that using his last name would sound more authoritative. Not that I held authority over him, but I needed to sound confident and strong. He would not be the reason I failed at my job all spring. "It wasn't really a question."

Everyone looked my way again, heads turning like they synchronized it, with surprised looks on their faces. No one was more surprised than Kace, and I could see him moving his legs uncomfortably as I got closer to the table.

"Actually, *Princess*, you don't understand. I don't need any PT. If I do need it, I'll let Gary know."

Oh no, he didn't. Where did he get off calling me Princess? No one called me princess. Not in that context, and not in that tone.

Kace must have seen the shift in me because I heard him mutter, "Oh shit."

Leaning into Chase, closer than I wanted to, I paused, snarled, and…sniffed? I freaking sniffed. Dang he smelled so good. Like clean, earthy musk. He hadn't been to work out yet for the day and was still dressed in the athletic shorts and a t-shirt he wore daily to and from the hotel.

What the hell was wrong with me? I was losing my train of thought, and he noticed because whatever he saw on my face made him smirk at me.

No. No. No.

Backing away quickly, I said the first thing I could think to say, which may have been the biggest lie I had ever told. "You stink."

He smiled like he knew I was just trying to save face, but he didn't call me out. Instead, he let the smile drop from his face and shrugged. "Go away, then."

At that point, our interaction had become a show for the others. Cards were dropped, and all eyes were on our exchange, waiting for what was coming next. I didn't want to be there anymore, but I refused to lose the battle we had engaged in.

"Okay, then. I will see you out there in fifteen minutes."

"Out where?"

"The field. If you won't come to me, I'll come to you."

"That isn't necessary, Princess." *More of that patronizing nickname.*

"Actually, it is, *Pancake*." *Pancake? Really Becca? Freaking Pancake?*

Okay. So, name-calling wasn't my strong suit. I would work on that.

"What is it you don't understand?" he asked, suppressing a laugh at my use of a breakfast dish to insult him. "If I say I'm fine, I'm fine. You're new here, but that's the way this works. I've been doing this longer than you've known what a boner is, so back off."

Kace started to move his chair and stand up, drawing the line at one of the guys talking to me that way. Or more likely the use of the word 'boner." But I could handle it. If Chase thought being crude could scare me away, it wouldn't work, so I eyed Kace to let me handle it.

"Okay, *Butter Boy*, I'll just write what I see in the report Gary asked me to turn in." I suppressed a cringe at my new nickname attempt, trying to own it even though it was ridiculous. All I knew was that butter was delicious on pancakes and Chase was making me crazy.

He hardly acknowledged the name that time, though. His face went white, and he started shifting uncomfortably. He knew I saw him; he knew I noticed his struggle. I let it go all week because I assumed he was seeing one of the other interns or trainers about it. Instead, as it turned out, he was just an idiot.

Turning to leave without waiting for a response, I grabbed my phone and shot Ali a quick text.

> Tell Kace to stand down. I got this.

> Got what?

> Just deliver my message, and I will fill you in when we talk tonight.

> Oooookaaaaay

Slipping my phone back into my pocket, I entered the training room where all the other interns were wrapping ankles and elbows.

Manny was waiting on me at a table, needing my help stretching out. He was Chase's backup but would be the new starter if something ever happened to Chase. Which was looking pretty promising, considering I was thinking about poking his damn eyes out.

Manny and I began his routine as he shouted around the room, acting like a tool. He was a nice enough guy but was cockier than he should have been. He was the backup, not the star, and he made me want to roll my eyes the whole time we worked together.

After Manny left, one of the other guys approached with a blister. Another with a sore neck. Another with a fever that had to be sent back to the hotel and quarantined until he was better.

Before I knew it, two hours had passed, and it was time to head to the field for the day's workout. I filled a waist pack full of small medical supplies—ointments, band-aids, and gauze—and snapped it onto my waist. By the time I was ready, the entire training room had been cleared and I headed toward the door as Chase made his way in.

"You win, Princess."

"Gary is on the field," I motioned, in case he was looking for him. I was done with him for the day, and needed to get past him to head to the field.

"I'm not looking for Gary. What do you need me to do?"

"Gary wants a check-up on you to start the season. He hasn't seen you in here all week. That's my job." Explaining to him what he already knew was pointless, but it had to be said.

"Well, I did tell you I was fine, didn't I?" He looked at me like what he said was the truth, and I should accept it. But we both knew it was a lie.

"Yes, but unfortunately, I can't write in a report: *'Said he's fine'.*"

"Get it over with then," he sighed heavily.

"Did my threat to follow you to the field scare you that much?" I quipped.

"Nope. What do you want?"

Liar.

"For you to stop calling me Princess," I started.

"Okay, Cupcake."

"I mean it, Dickhead. I am not losing this job opportunity because of what I lack between my legs. And your little nick-names are demeaning here."

"As opposed to...?" he led.

"As opposed to what?"

"You said my nicknames are demeaning *here*, where would they not be? We can go there instead."

Oh, for the love of carrot cake.

"You know what I meant, Asshole."

"How come you get to name-call?"

"Because your job isn't on the line," I fired back, practically yelling. Why was I giving him that much insight? He didn't need to know my weakness.

But he didn't respond, just straightened his stance and looked off at something random on the wall to his right. While he wasn't looking at me, I took the chance to look at him.

Since I'd left him in the locker room, he had changed into his uniform. I wouldn't be human if I didn't notice how it hugged his muscular body and had a tattoo peeking from below one of his sleeves. His scruffy and strong jawline was ticking in frustration. His hat was pulled low over his dark brown eyes. His hands were on his hips.

It was a serious challenge to not drool as I took him in. Gary had said ogling the players was *inappropriate*. But surely, he didn't mean Chase. Because Chase was a man among boys inside that locker room and on the field. Despite his sour attitude and ability to make me want to stab him, he was perfectly sculpted and obviously sexy. There was no chance of me not ogling a little, especially since I had been crushing on him since I was fourteen.

That was how old I was when he first joined the league. Even though he hadn't spent all those years with the Kings, I saw him on all the sports channels. Then when he signed with Atlanta, Cam and Kace befriended him. They never said much about him, though, and I didn't ask. But I continued to follow his career as a fan.

"Okay," he interrupted my thoughts with the one word I didn't think he knew.

"Okay?" My eyes shot up, confused about what the question was at first. *Oh yeah, his baseline.*

"Do a physical and then be done. Deal?"

I hesitantly nodded, still unsure why a routine physical was freaking him out. "Now?"

"Tomorrow."

"I have to have the report in by tomorrow," I stressed.

"Then I'll meet you here tonight right after practice. But not now. Ethan is in the bullpen waiting on a catcher."

"I'll be here," I said nicely as he walked out.

When I took that job, unruly players were the last thing I anticipated being an issue. Especially veterans such as Chase. Athletes wanted to take care of their bodies, and trainers were the catalyst to help them see that through. We were the good guys.

So, I absolutely, one hundred percent, fully expected to find Chase in that training room after everyone else cleared out that night. I never doubted for a minute that he would show up because he knew he needed me just as much as I needed him in order to be successful.

But when it was ten p.m., I had been waiting for four hours.

I missed dinner.

I was tired.

I had been working all day.

My clothes were rumpled.

My feet hurt.

My brain was on the blink.

And that bastard still wasn't there.

I didn't know why I trusted him to show or help me, help him. But I knew one thing for absolute certain.

Chase Turner was a stupid, fucking liar.

chase

"DAD? WHAT ARE YOU DOING HERE?" I WAS CALLED OUT OF THE locker room after practice by security. They told me someone was outside the door claiming to be my father and asked if I would check it out since the man was so insistent.

Then there he was, my drunk ass father. In Florida, at the stadium.

"Can't an old man come to see his son play?"

"No, Dad, they can't. Not when they can't put down a liquor bottle long enough to function," I snapped, anger coming off me in waves.

"Nonsense. I haven't dranken in 3… whole… minutes," he laughed, with a slur in his words.

"How did you even get here from Atlanta? I paid my housekeeper double to help you and keep an eye on you. Why come here?" I was leading my dad away from the locker room door, walking down a corridor the grounds crew used, hoping to hide from anyone who may pass by.

"I drove your fancy car," Dad shrugged.

"You drove?" I hissed, nearly losing it all together. "You thought a seven hour drive was a good idea?"

"Your car is fine, son."

"I'm not worried about the car!"

"I'm fine, son."

"I'm not worried about you, either!" I yelled even louder, my voice echoing off the walls around me. "You could have killed someone. Maybe you already did! Where's the damn car?"

"I had trouble parking it, so I left it in a safe spot."

"Where. Is. The car?" I repeated evenly. My tone was almost lethal. I didn't even know which of my five cars he had. I'd flown down with a few of the guys to avoid the hassle of having a car there at all but I should have brought all the keys with me.

I didn't want his problems to infiltrate my game. It was important to me to keep it separate and deal with it. So I needed to get him out of there immediately and mitigate the damage. Without even changing my clothes or saying goodbye, I grabbed my dad's elbow and pulled him toward the exit.

Luckily, I had kept my phone in my hand when I walked out, so I had it with me. That way, I was able to order an Uber, and we got across town at a hotel in no time. Once we were there, Dad passed out and arranged to get him back to Atlanta the following day.

My mother had died a couple of years ago, which was when my Dad started drinking so heavily. I was also an only child. I didn't have cousins or uncles. No living grandparents. It was up to me and me alone to handle my dad. But up until the end of last season, he was a functioning drunk. That didn't mean it was okay, but he was his own problem, not mine. Now, I didn't know what to do with him.

All I knew was I was going to put him on a plane the next morning and have my housekeeper pick him up at the airport. *I was going to have to triple her salary.*

Once I made sure Dad was nice and passed the fuck out, I called another Uber to drive me around and help me find my car. After an $86 fare and a $300 tip, I found my Maserati Levante—

my favorite—double parked at a grocery store close to the stadium. There was a dent on the driver's side front fender and chances were, I would never find out what happened because he wouldn't remember.

The keys had been left in the ignition and the car was unlocked, so I should have been thankful it was still there. Hopping in, I cranked it up and looked around at the inside to assess the damage. Luckily, nothing stood out except receipts from five different liquor stores in the console to which I angrily tossed them in the back to get them out of sight.

Since the car was there, I decided to use it and drive it home after spring training was over. Hopefully, no one would question how it got there, but if they did, I would just lie and tell them I had it brought down.

Before driving back to my dad's hotel, I took the chance that he would be passed out for the rest of the night and decided to go to my own hotel for a shower and a change of clothes. Using the shower's hot water, I tried to loosen up my muscles and ease the tension in my shoulders. The stress was so heavy that I almost forgot I had knee pain. The shower was helping, though, and I was finally letting the drama of the day go when I heard a pounding from the main room.

Then the noise was gone.

Then it was back.

Someone was at the door, and it sounded urgent.

For the love of all things baseball, please don't be about my dad.

Grabbing a towel, I threw it quickly around my waist, and ran for the door without drying off. In case it was my dad, I readied myself to pull him into the room before anyone saw him.

But it wasn't my dad.

It wasn't even about my dad.

It was Becca. And she was pissed.

Worse than pissed.

"Oh shit," I muttered. It dawned on me that I was supposed to meet her. Something I had forgotten about once my dad showed up.

Becca was still in her work clothes, her hair was in a messy bun, her shoes were in her hand, and her eyes were angry. I'm not sure I had ever seen anything sexier in my life.

"Oh shit? Is that all you have to say?" she yelled, breaking my lust-filled trance.

"Keep it down," I warned.

"Do you not realize what it's like to be a woman in this business? Do you not realize how small matters like 'not turning in a simple check up on the team's number one catcher' affect me? This is a man's world and I have to be respected to be successful and you are fucking it all up. Gary wants a report to start the season, I told him no problem. But guess what, *Princess*? You're screwing this up for me."

Holding my towel with one hand, I pulled her into my room with the other, shutting the door so the whole complex didn't hear. She stumbled from the sudden force, and once she righted herself, she realized I was in my towel, and she was in my room.

"What are you doing?" she asked like she wasn't the one who knocked on my door and yelled at me.

"I was showering before Lady Goliath showed up at my door, so this is what you get, Crazy Kingkiller." I had a hard time keeping a straight face. She didn't like Princess or Cupcake, but calling her Crazy Kingkiller didn't seem to sit well either. I wasn't sure where the hell I pulled that name out from, I just knew I refused to call her Becca. Becca made her too tempting.

"I'm outta here!" she yelled, starting to scramble toward the door.

Grabbing her elbow, I whirled her back around to face me. "Oh no, you don't."

I was playing with fire. I was so damn hot for that woman that it made me two kinds of mad. Plus, I was naked, and she was over there losing her shit on me. The combination of it all was bound to make things entirely too challenging.

Instead of keeping her there, I should have let her leave. She could go stew in anger alone while I returned to my dad. It just didn't go that way.

"I didn't mean to upset you or stand you up, but something came up." I was starting with the truth, but I knew the rest would be a lie. "Someone hit my car in the parking lot and I got distracted taking care of it. By the time that was done, I figured you were long gone. Please don't tell me you waited all this time."

"Are you okay?" Her concern was a sudden whiplash in her demeanor.

"I am," I replied carefully, worried she would whip right back into *Lady Goliath*. "I wasn't in the car, I just had to file a report and all."

"Okay, okay." She nodded, accepted my dishonest words as a logical excuse, and calmed down.

"What about right now?" *What the hell are you doing, Turner?*

"What right now?"

"Check me over," I suggested. *Bad idea, bad idea.*

"That is a bad idea," she repeated the thoughts in my head.

"It is a very bad idea," I confirmed. "But it will get us what we both want. You get to make Gary happy; I get to get it over with."

"What's the big deal, Chase? You've played for ten years. Are you scared of getting your reflexes tapped?"

I scoffed and shook my head. "No." *Yes.* "What's it gonna be, Kingkiller?"

"Can you put shorts on first?"

"Nah." I had intended to until she asked. Something about her made me want to make her as uncomfortable as she made me.

Hopping on the desk, I sat and dangled my legs, my feet coming only inches from the floor. It could be our makeshift training table, but my towel had slightly opened and was barely doing the job I had assigned it to do.

I didn't move to fix it, though. I stayed steadfast in my attempt to be difficult.

Becca turned away and wiped a hand down her face, muttering something to herself that I couldn't make out. The only word I caught was the word 'stupid.'

Once she got herself together, she looked around the room before walking quickly to the bathroom. When she came back, she had my brush in her hand. Then, she went to the bedside table drawer and grabbed a pen and a notepad. She picked up my watch from the dresser and studied it for a minute, then nodded a little as if it would do. Lastly, she went to the mini bar and pulled a cup from its plastic container.

I could almost guess what most of that was for, but the cup? "I'm not peeing in that, Princess."

"I'm a trainer, not a specimen collector, Pancake." She looked at me like I had lost my mind, then opened the minibar and poured an entire shot of vodka into the cup. As she downed it in one gulp, I cringed, the act reminding me I needed to get back to my dad.

But I understood her need for liquor. Had I not needed to drive across town to my drunk father, I'd have joined her. If there was ever a time for shots, it was then.

Becca had dropped her shoes when she walked in and her feet were still bare, which made my heart race as she padded across the carpeted floor toward me. She used the brush to tap my knees, causing me to wince, but not enough to make her suspicious. Then, she wrote a few things down on the pad of paper.

"Stand up," she requested when she was done.

I did so without a word, hoping to not prolong the torture.

"Spread your arms wide."

Ensuring my towel was tucked tight, I lifted my arms straight out to the sides, creating a T. Becca licked her lips and muttered more words before lifting her hands to my shoulders.

Once her soft fingers made contact, I involuntarily shuttered, making her withdraw her hands quickly. She stared for a minute, trying to determine what was happening.

"Your hands are cold," I lied again.

"No, they're not," she objected, calling me out and continuing her assessment. With her hands back on me, she rubbed them across my shoulders and squeezed. "Any pain?"

"No."

Slowly, her hands moved from my shoulders to my arms and then squeezed my biceps, making me wince.

"Hurt?"

"No." The pain wasn't the problem. It was her hands on my body as I stood there naked in a private room. The temptation was unbearable.

When she bit her lip and batted her lashes at me, I wondered if she realized how her touch affected me. I also wondered why she had to be so damn beautiful.

Once she ensured my arms muscles and reflexes were tested, she did the unthinkable and fell to her knees in front of me.

Okay, she didn't fall, she squatted gracefully. But you couldn't tell my cock she wasn't there for him. And with her hair looking like I had just used it as a handle, I had to suppress another groan and look at the ceiling before I embarrassed myself.

When her hands touched my ankles, I exhaled hard and looked back down at her, unable to turn away. Slowly—way-too-fucking-slowly—she brought her hands upward, squeezing my calf muscles as she went.

Why was this happening?

Becca's movements didn't feel like a medical workup. They felt like foreplay. As her hands squeezed the muscles in my calves, I forgot all about my knees. Closing my eyes, I tried to picture something else, something revolting, and use that image to save myself from the situation I had gotten myself into. A contest I thought I could win but was losing by the second as my cock stood at attention.

With one point of pressure to the tendons below my kneecaps, I opened my eyes and winced, a noise that was less turned on and more pain. She nailed the source of all my fear and once I twisted in obvious discomfort, she stood up quickly, not looking out for anything above her.

Which was when her head hit my hard cock, barely covered by the towel, and embarrassment flooded my veins. Fuck, it couldn't get any worse.

Stepping back, I grabbed myself, trying to protect my dick from her assault and also hide what had become so obvious. That I was turned on and losing control of myself. Meanwhile, she jumped back, holding her head like my dick was made of steel, and she was in danger of a concussion. Her eyes were wide, and her face was red.

I wasn't sure who was more appalled, but neither of us turned around. We simply kept our eyes on one another as the shock settled between us. I knew I had to do or say something to break the spell.

"You done?" I bit at her sharply.

"Your knee," she mentioned, her eyes still trained on my face.

"You need to leave."

"Yeah, I really, really, really do. But your knee needs..."

"Nope."

"Chase..." she warned.

I knew what she was thinking. She was going to report the knee pain to Gary. Gary would then call me in for scans. Scans would show tears. Tears would sideline me. Manny Fucking Fernandez would become the new starting catcher for the Atlanta Kings.

No-fucking-thank you.

becca

STORMING OUT OF CHASE'S ROOM, HUMILIATION TOOK HOLD OF MY body. I wasn't naïve enough to think that feeling all over his body while he was naked in a towel was a good idea. We even both established beforehand that it was a bad, bad idea.

In any other context, maybe those conditions would have led two available and willing adults into each other's arms. Maybe into the bed. Making each other feel and forget everything that had them so worked up to begin with.

But we were working.

It was our job.

And I had been so desperate to finish my reports for Gary that I let myself get reckless. I'd bet my entire shoe collection that Chase knew what he was doing and was making me crazy. He probably hoped I would rush through and overlook any issues if he spun me up enough. And it almost worked. Running so fast out of that room, I hadn't bothered finishing my assessment. I didn't check his vitals or even take my notes. But being in the safety of my own room gave me a chance to think clearly, and I knew what I had to do.

Even though I didn't have a report to send Gary, I did have

some insight on Chase Turner. He was a catcher, and catchers notoriously had leg and knee issues. The first day I saw him catching for Ethan Jones, I saw the pain written on his face. Each squat hindered his ability to react to balls thrown in the dirt, or too far off the plate. It was my job to recognize that and get him well. Not just for his sake but also for the sake of the team. He shouldn't have been fighting me on it, either. We should have been working together to get him ready for the regular season.

At the rate we were going, Fernandez would definitely be the opening-day starting catcher, even without me poking Chase's eyes out, which I was tempted to do every time I saw him. And as much as I believed Fernandez could handle the job, he wasn't Chase Turner. As a longtime fan, I wanted Chase behind the plate.

Gary and the manager would have to temporarily bench him the second they heard what I had to say. If he didn't get himself right, the effects could be a detriment to the team. So, with my mind made up, I texted Gary that I needed to meet with him first thing in the morning about one of the catchers needing knee scans, and went to bed.

Sleep didn't come easily. I spent all night replaying how I felt when Chase opened that door in only a towel. I kept seeing his hard body, and the drops of water from his shower that ran down the planes of his tanned muscles. His chest had just enough hair to show me how all grown up he was, and his tattoo was entirely visible–a vintage baseball with slashes through it. His hair was a sexy, wet mess. His eyes were wide, surprised to see me there.

When I got to his door, I was mad at him, but I was even angrier at myself for being unable to control how I responded to him.

Chase saw it.

That was why he tried unhinging me.

That was why Gary had warned me away on my first day.

That was why he singled me out.

I had bitten back about me ogling the players, yet he had been right, and I was proving him righter by the second. How predictable that a female, working close to the players, couldn't see past her own lust to do her job correctly?

Sighing, I flipped over, and covered my head with my pillow. No one but me knew I had that conversation with myself. No one but me knew how close I was to breaking the rules only a week into the job.

Determined to get right, I vowed that when I woke up, I would be more resolute, and back to being the girl that showed up to kick ass. Chase wasn't going to turn me into someone I wasn't.

Chase was already sitting on a training table when I walked in the following day. He knew Gary would call him when his scans were scheduled, and I didn't ask him to be there, so other than trying to make me crazier than I was, I couldn't find a reason for his presence. He wasn't talking to anyone. Not even his teammates as they all started filing in for the day. He just sat quietly on the training table until I finished what I was doing and headed to him.

"What are you doing here?" I asked skeptically, hoping I was strong enough not to fall victim to any lies he might try telling me. "I haven't had a chance to report to Gary yet this morning."

"Just trying to save you from having to track me down," he shrugged. "Ready to get this over with."

"I'm sure Gary will call you when he gets my report."

"Oh, I know. This isn't my first rodeo."

"Then why be here now?"

"What else am I going to do? My knees are shot to hell, Princess. Now that you know, it makes no sense to make it worse."

"I'm confused about why this is such a big deal." That was the wrong thing to say, but I only realized it after it came out. Ballplayers ate and breathed baseball. Of course it was a big deal. In his eyes, I could see that he was about to snap at me again, so I stopped him by rephrasing myself. "What I mean is… wouldn't you rather get this fixed than lie and let it linger?"

Chase shook his head solemnly. "Not this year."

"Becca!" I heard my name shouted behind me, making Chase and I both look up to see who it was.

Manny Fernandez.

"Hey, are you ready for your wraps?" I asked nicely. Nicer than I had ever been to Chase.

"Yeah, let's do this." As he approached the table next to Chase, he nodded and started taunting him, which was not new among them. "What are you doing here, Old Man? Thought you were fine."

Chase normally jabbed at him back, but when he stayed quiet, I got a little pissed at Manny on Chase's behalf. He had no idea Chase was in the middle of turmoil with his knees and he needed to stop pushing.

"Hey Grandpa," Manny started again at Chase. "Why so quiet? Teeth fall out?"

Calm down, Becca, this is what they do. This was how they showed their friendship. Boys are weird.

Chase continued to stay quiet.

"Okay, Mr. Geriatric, be a punk-ass little bitch." Whoa. Manny took that one step further than my brain could comprehend. "I'll be out there backstopping for Ethan if you decide you want to back me up."

How was Chase just sitting there?

Say something, Pancake, say something.

He didn't, just stared at Manny impassively.

"Actually, Fernandez," I raised a finger to get his attention and braced myself for what I was about to say. "I sent Gary a request to have your knees x-rayed. He's on his way in. You need to wait for him to clear you."

Yep, I lied.

"The fuck?" he yelled, crowding into me.

Flinching at his anger–his very justified outrage–I tried to hold my lie together. As far as I knew, Manny was completely healthy. But I had told Gary that one of the catchers needed scans and didn't tell him who. Thanks to Fernandez pissing me off, he was that guy. Because damn him.

I was being the opposite of a professional, but I had been kneeling in Chase's room the night before, so why stop there? *For the love of God, help me.*

"Watch your tone," Chase finally spoke up to Fernandez.

"Fuck off, man. I don't need any delays. I'm fine."

"Fine? I don't know about that," Chase scoffed tauntingly. "All I do know is you need to watch how you talk to her." His voice lowered with his last six words, and sounded downright menacing.

Chase hadn't exactly been a gentleman when he talked to me, so it was weird hearing him defend me to Manny with such vehemence.

"This is fucking insane," Fernandez yelled. "The only thing I need is a new fucking intern that knows what the fuck she's doing. Maybe there's a reason that pussy doesn't belong in this locker room. Bitches don't cut it here."

He wasn't wrong about me being insane because I was, indeed, insane. What possessed me to cut him off today and feed him to Gary? Especially when Chase needed the care.

Not that Chase was denying my lie. But maybe that was because he didn't have a chance. Fernandez wouldn't shut up long enough to let anyone else talk. And when Fernandez did get quiet, it was because he was on his back, on the ground, with blood running from his nose.

Shit.

While I had my minor panic attack, Chase had hit Manny. Chase was shaking his hand out and giving Manny the death glare from hell as he stood over the top of him.

"Chase!" I yelled. But he wasn't even considering me. He was leaning down, closer to Manny. "Don't you ever talk to her, or anyone else, like that again."

"Fuck you, man. What's your fucking problem?" Manny pushed at him, trying to get up.

"All she's trying to do is her goddamn job. She doesn't need guys like you making it harder."

Where the hell was the old Chase? Didn't I give him that same speech? Didn't he give me the same shit?

Of course, he didn't call me a *bitch.*

Wiping my hand down my face in frustration, I realized we had caused a scene. My lie had turned into chaos. No one came to Manny's aid, though. No one tried to get in between him and Chase. Everyone just crossed their arms, watching, waiting to see what happened next.

Including Gary.

Including Kace.

Chase could do whatever he wanted, but I couldn't stomach being in a circle of all those guys staring back. They were all very pissed off guys and I couldn't tell if they were upset with Chase, Manny, or me. I just knew I had to get out of there.

Passing Gary on the way out, I mumbled, "Fernandez needs those scans I told you about. I will give Chase's evaluation to you in a bit."

Gary quietly nodded while keeping his eye on the scene but I didn't bother looking back. I didn't care if Chase was still in Manny's face or if he let him get up. I was too busy being mortified and mad—at myself. One little comment got under my skin and I told a bold face lie out of spite.

When Manny's scans came back clean, I knew I would be able to talk my way out of why I recommended them, but if I admitted I lied, all of that would have been for nothing, and I would be out of there. So I headed to the office, where I knew I could sit for a while, and gather myself. I could work on paperwork and avoid everyone for a little bit.

Gary's desk was the main piece in the office, but there was a couch and a few small desks that we could use when needed. When I walked in, I shut the door behind me and began pacing the room from the entrance back to Gary's desk.

After about ten laps, I heard the door open behind me and I turned back expecting to see Gary. Chase was leaning on the door jam, arms crossed, with a sly look on his face. His hand had an ice wrap, and he had dressed out in his uniform.

"Welcome to the dark side, Cupcake," he raised one eyebrow at me.

Shaking my head in disbelief, I let the nickname slide. It beat the hell out of being called a *bitch*.

"I cannot believe I said that. I cannot believe I lied." Then I looked at his hand and back to his face. "I cannot believe you hit him."

He pushed himself from the doorway and entered the office with one step and another smirk. "Hey, you defended my honor, so I defended yours."

That got a tiny laugh out of me, but I didn't respond.

Chase reached behind him and shut the door to the office, closing us in—alone once again.

Immediately, I started heating up at the reminder of being alone in his room. He was fully dressed in his uniform instead of a towel, but he was no less sexy. His uniform fit like a glove, tucked in and showing off his trim waist that I knew led to a broad muscled chest underneath the jersey. The pants were tight on his thighs and cuffed at his knees, showing off his high socks —an old-school look that practically made me swoon.

I must have stared too long because Chase's loud "ahem" brought my eyes back to his face, and the smile on his lips told me he knew where my head had gone. I turned away from him to hide my reddened face and take a deep breath.

"I don't know what to do," I confessed. "Are you going to tell Gary I lied?"

"Depends."

"On?"

"On if you want to stay on the dark side with me."

The look of confusion on my face spoke volumes, but I asked for an explanation anyway. "You're going to have to be more specific."

"Well, my original plan was to fake it until I couldn't. Now, my plan is to have you treat my knees, off the record."

"I can't do that!" I said, turning my back to him and throwing my arms in the air.

"Sure, you can. Neither one of us wants to get busted. I want to play; you want the job. It's perfect."

"I don't even know what's wrong, Chase. You need an MRI or an X-ray. That isn't my job. I'm not that person."

As I began to pace again, he walked in closer, hands up placatingly, and stopped my strides. "They fucking hurt. I don't need a cure; I just want to play. Make the pain bearable."

That man was certifiably insane. We had more in common than I thought. "I could just tell Gary that you also need to be seen."

"No, you can't. Because then I will have to tell Gary you lied about Fernandez. And Gary's reaction will be the least of your problems. Fernandez will be the issue."

Would he really throw me under the bus? Gary would fire me. But even if he didn't, Chase had a point. I didn't want to stir any more shit up with Manny, that was for damn sure.

Ugh.

I was going to do it.

I knew I was.

Not only because I dug my own grave but because I selfishly wanted Chase to play. Not to mention I didn't want to give Manny the satisfaction of calling me a bitch, and then proven how right he was.

"Manny had every right to call me whatever he wanted, I straight up lied about his health, Chase. I feel awful."

"Actually, Princess. That motherfucker deserved more than one punch to his face. He's a jackass. Maybe this is karma for some of the shit he pulls. You haven't even seen the real Manny Fernandez, yet. And, for the record, no one ever has the right to call you a bitch."

"The whole team looked so mad at me for causing a scene, though." My mind drifted to the look on their faces.

"The whole team doesn't know you caused any trouble. As far as they know, you were doing your job and Fernandez couldn't handle it. They were mad at him for the way he talked to you. Trust me."

Talking things out was making my nerves ebb a little. Chase was right. He and I were the only ones who knew the whole story, and as long as I kept his secret, he would keep mine.

"Fine. Meet me here tonight and I'll try to figure out what to do with your knees. But remember, Chase, I'm not a doctor. I can only give you a band-aid, not an antidote."

"I know," he said matter-of-fact.

"And, if you are a no show, again, I get to send you to Gary, and you have to keep your mouth shut."

"Deal, Cupcake."

"And stop calling me that."

"Deal... Princess."

chase

After Becca had run out of my hotel room the night before, I had to take another shower—with cold water. There was no way I could leave my room and get back to my dad until I was settled back down. It took a solid hour, but eventually, I made it and stayed with Dad so I could get him on an early flight back to Atlanta.

Then, I went straight to the complex and waited for Becca to deliver the news to Gary. There was no sense worrying about my lack of sleep when I would be sent back to rest anyway. But Becca changed the whole game in the blink of an eye.

When she told Fernandez he was getting *my* knee scans, I wanted to marry that woman. And no motherfucker like Fernandez was going to talk about my future wife the way he did.

So I hit him, and it felt good.

Besides talking to Becca the way he had, he was a dick. His mouth never stopped moving, and he always had some shit to say about someone else. He went beyond typical locker room banter and didn't know when to stop.

Every guy in that room who saw me hit him wished it was them—coaches included. No one blamed me for snapping. We may have been a bunch of jocks, but none of us believed in demeaning anyone—especially women.

Especially women that worked for the organization.

Sure, I had given Becca a ton of shit, and I honestly planned on giving her more. Especially since she was my very own personal physical therapist. We were going to be spending a lot of time together. With her help, I was hopeful I could get through the season.

But I would be lying if I didn't consider being a no-show to our first meet-up. A small part of me wanted her to appear at my door again, wild and unhinged, with her hair twisted up and eyes blazing with rage.

I wanted *that* Becca again. I wanted to see her on her knees, touching me…

"Hello?"

Shit.

Snapping out of la-la land, I sat on the training table in the darkened room, waiting for her to come around the corner. She appeared in the doorway and I smiled, trying not to scare her away before we even got started.

"Hey, Prin… Cupcake. Wait, I forgot which one you said I couldn't call you." The lights were on a timed system and because the stadium was technically closed, they were off. The emergency lights were all we had, but even in the dimness, I could still see her roll her eyes at me.

"You're early," she looked at me warily, disregarding my nicknames.

"Making amends for being late last time."

"You weren't late, you never showed."

"Eh, tomatoes, tomahtoes."

"I cannot believe I'm doing this," she groaned as she set her bag on the table beside me. "Let's get this over with."

When I wasn't in uniform, I wore athletic shorts and a t-shirt. Therefore, my attire gave her safe access to my legs and knees, without having to pull my pants off. It felt like a considerate thought on my part. There was less of a chance that my cock would get uncontrollably hard with my pants on.

Or so I thought.

"Scoot back on the table so that your knees are straight. I'm going to feel around for any abnormalities. Let me know where you feel the most pain."

She softly put her hands on each of my shins, pressing slightly as each one made its way up to my knees. Under her soft touch, I shuddered and bit my lip, realizing that it didn't matter what I wore. Her delicate hands were the main factor in my libidinous situation.

Because I was instantly hard again.

My body was begging me to grab her and pull her to me. Just a little taste, a small touch. Anything that could ease the need she instilled in me as she marked my skin.

"Okay?" She paused, realizing I had stopped breathing.

"Yep," I nodded curtly.

She started again, inching her way up, keeping her eyes on mine like she was looking for my next lie. Right as she got underneath my kneecap, I felt it.

Pain.

Wincing, I pulled back and she lifted her hands to give me space. Because of our first full squad practice, and with Fernandez being out for the day, I was extra sore. Not to mention I had barely slept.

"That's the spot, Princess. It feels strained. I normally get a little pain at the beginning of each season, but this is more severe." Honesty was all I gave her. She needed that from me if she was going to do her job.

"Did anything happen during the offseason?"

And just like that, I was back to lying. "No. I just didn't work out the way I normally do."

"Why?"

"I don't know why. I just didn't."

She huffed, causing a stray hair that had fallen in front of her face to lift as she exhaled. Becca was giving my words some thought, but eventually continued to evaluate my legs, poking, prodding, and asking easier questions.

After a few more minutes, she pinched the bridge of her nose and shook her head. "Most likely, your cartilage through here has broken down. Through the years, you have put more and more pressure on your tendons. It's a common injury for catchers, but the pain is usually avoidable with a steady exercise regimen. I assume you've always had a routine to keep your body in shape, correct?"

"Yeah," I blinked, looking at my knees like they betrayed me.

"This is the type of thing that can lead to muscle damage and life-long mobility problems if not treated."

"What if they're torn?" A torn ligament scared the fuck out of me.

"Honestly, there's a chance they could be separating from the bone, but that isn't something I can see with my eyes. I need scans for that, asshole." Calling me an asshole was fair enough. Afterall, I was asking her to use her nonexistent X-ray vision to give me a diagnosis.

"And that is not an option during the spring, under the team doctors," I shook my head. "So what now?"

"Well, you need to do a stretching regimen every morning and most nights. Also, stretching properly after the game will be necessary as well to help the muscles wind down. I will help you in the mornings and at night to ensure a full range of motion and proper technique. Ice to decrease swelling and increase blood flow. Heat. Wraps. All of those will also be necessary. Your core looks strong, and I know you have standard stretches before the games, but you can't limit your stretching to the knees. Quads, hips, and gluteus exercises will help balance your strength and take the pressure off your knees. After a couple of weeks, hopefully, the pain will be tolerable."

She was in the zone, steadfast and confident as she spoke. All I could do was stare at how hot she looked when she was studious with an underlying fluster. When she stopped talking, she made eye contact while waiting for my response. But I just kept staring.

Her beautiful face held only a hint of make-up, her lashes were long, her eyes deep blue. She gave me a sense of familiarity, but I knew I had never seen someone that called to me the way she had. Under the dim lights of the room and with her hands on me, I wanted to lean in and kiss her, touch her. But despite how many lines she was crossing for me, I couldn't push her to cross another one.

"Okay, Princess," I whispered. "Let's do it."

My words broke the trance we had both been in and she nodded. To put distance between us, she backed up and I wondered if she felt what I was feeling. Like for a fraction of a second, crossing another line would be worth it.

We planned to meet in my room early before we had to report to work. She was going to do as much as she could away from the complex so there was no danger in someone seeing what we were doing. After the days were over and the complex cleared out, we could meet in the training room and use the equipment and supplies if we needed to.

She made me promise that I would also come to her during practices and games if I needed something. If I kept avoiding her, it looked apparent that something was wrong. Gary would take notice, just like he did when she couldn't get a check-up with me, and neither of us wanted Gary's attention.

Once we were done for the night, we shared an Uber to the hotel. If anyone saw us, we could pass the session off as that check-up she promised Gary. But no one was around by the time we got back.

We shared an elevator ride up to her floor, and before she got off, I stopped the elevator and kept the doors closed, breathing in and out as calmly as possible.

"Thanks, Becca." My sincerity surprised her, or maybe it was the use of her real name. She didn't respond. She just hit the button again for the doors to open and walked out, leaving me reeling.

becca

I barely slept. I didn't eat. I was a zombie by the time I made it to Chase's room the following morning. The earlier wake-up call would take getting used to, but in a way, I was also excited. Chase had become my own personal project, and I loved the challenge he gave me.

Before I could even knock on Chase's door, he opened it and quickly ushered me in. He wore shorts but no shirt, his hair was messy, and his feet were bare. I followed him into the space of the room that had a couch and chair near the sliding doors to his balcony, but they had been pushed toward the walls to make room on the floor.

It was still dark outside, so his lamps were our only light, but it was enough. He turned around and asked me what I needed him to do, so I fought my urge to just stare and started instructing him on where to lay and how to bend.

In order to get the most out of the stretches, I leaned on him and pushed his legs. He groaned and breathed into each move-ment, making the hairs on my neck stand up, and my stomach flip with ardor. He was taking the exercise extremely seriously, and I was thankful for the intense side of Chase Turner.

But he was inadvertently drawing me in, making me want him in a way I knew was wrong. It was more than just a crush. The way he took my commands and occasionally locked eyes with me was creating something else inside of me.

Once we were done, he stood, and I noticed him adjusting himself, obviously trying to hide his erection. I had to turn around quickly to hide that I saw him, but of course, Chase noticed and couldn't let it go.

"Look, Princess, let's just go ahead and clear the air here. I find you extremely attractive. And with you feeling my legs up and laying over top of me while I stretch, I'm going to have more boners than you're probably comfortable with. I'm only human."

His matter-of-fact vulgarity made me laugh, and I was able to face him and nod. My arousal wasn't as obvious, but it was there, and I would be a hypocrite if I scoffed at his honesty.

"Just keeping it real," he smiled.

"Fair enough, Turner," I conceded while stuffing my things back into the bag I carried.

When I left, I walked quickly back to my room to get my work clothes on and get down to the shuttle. It was still fairly early, so I had time to grab some coffee and text Ali since she was always up early.

This is harder than I thought it would be.
Knowing how to do your job and making "pro" decisions are two different things.

Bigger than high school, huh?

These guys live for this game. It's everything to them. Something as dumb as knees can cause so much drama.

Ohhhh are you talking about Fernandez?

Of course Kace told her what happened. Even though I had technically been referring to Chase and the drama he and I had between us. But she didn't need to know that much, yet.

Um, yeah. It was crazy.

According to Kace, Fernandez lucked out.

How so?

Chase hit him before Kace could.

Yeah, he was pretty mad.

Cam said he owes Chase a beer when we get there.

Well, he better come up with another reason to suggest that to Chase. I'm still on the down-low around here.

But other than that, I take it you and Chase made up?

What? Sorta. Shit, I couldn't tell her that, either. I loved my best friend, but she would tell Kace everything—or worse, my brother. And something told me they wouldn't take too kindly to the shit I caused among the catchers.

Not really. He still hates me for some reason. But I guess he draws the line at some things.

Sure. Sure. ;-)

I rolled my eyes and closed the text out, done with that crazy woman for a while. Since we had become so close, she had wanted me to have what she had. Commitment, love, and forever. She'd look for any reason to find something between

Chase and me if I gave her a hint that we were physically attracted to one another.

What Chase and I had was an understanding.

A truce.

That was it.

After arriving at the complex, Gary called me into his office. I was convinced he knew about Chase, and the lies I told about Manny. But instead of yelling at me, he congratulated me on my instincts.

Apparently, Manny had significant fluid buildup and had to have it drained. He hadn't even felt the effects yet, so I looked like a genius for figuring it out early. The irony had me laughing to myself the entire morning. Even giggling under my breath as I watched the game on the TV in the locker room.

"He's running!" the announcer yelled, getting my attention. "He's out!"

Chase threw out the attempted base stealer and the team started jogging off the field. The game was in the fourth inning, and since I wasn't needed much during the game, I was resting with my feet up, getting ready for the first wave of players to come in from the dugout.

Gary and his assistant were the only trainers in the dugout during games. So, when Gary's assistant, Troy, came into the locker room and called for me, I thought he was kidding.

"Becca, Gary is asking for you."

"Who me?"

"Is there another Becca in here?"

"Where does he need me?"

"In the dugout," he rolled his eyes and took off back down the hallway that led to the field. In the past week, I had been on the field numerous times, but never with a crowd of fans in the seats. My nerves started to rattle as I made my way down the hall, but I found a little peace knowing I was only going to the dugout, not the field.

"Becca," Gary barked as soon as I came into view. "Turner is coming out of the game. He said he's feeling some tightness after that throw. Follow him down the field and help him stretch it out."

Gary barely spared me a glance, just nodded toward the other end of the dugout. Looking down, I saw Chase taking his catcher's gear off and laughing with another player. He looked tired from four hard innings of baseball in the Florida heat, but he didn't appear to be in pain.

"Chop-chop," Gary growled, making me jump.

Chase hadn't looked like he was ready or even needed me, but I slowly started walking down the dugout toward him. As I passed Kace, he smirked like he knew I was walking toward my demise, and I gave him a forced smile. To his credit, he still hadn't acknowledged our friendship and made no exception in that moment, either. He just turned and started talking to the guys around him, letting me seal my own fate.

When I got close enough to Chase, I schooled my face with disinterest, hoping I looked less nervous than I was. "We need to stretch."

"The hell we do," he snorted, looking back with annoyance once he realized I was there.

"Gary called me out here because you said you felt tight on that last throw, let me do my job."

Be cool. Be calm.

"I can handle it."

Ah, he wanted to play that game. He wanted to act like we didn't have a deal and cause Gary to make my life hell when I couldn't deliver what he wanted me to do.

"I have to do as Gary requests." With wide eyes, I gave him my best "*do it*" look, but it didn't even phase him.

"Shoo, Princess," he flicked his fingers, then turned away.

Oh no he didn't.

"Chase, I swear to God, if you don't get your ass out there, I will rip your balls off and kick your kneecaps." I tried to keep my scornful tone low, so the whole dugout didn't hear me. "And stop calling me Princess."

Chase turned back, his eyes bugging out of his head in disbelief and a small smirk sitting on his perfect lips. The other guy Chase had been talking to, Keith Sanders, a new relief pitcher, was also looking at me like I had lost my damn mind. But I didn't care. I couldn't let Chase dismiss me, especially not in front of everyone.

As I stomped out of the dugout, I made my way down the foul area where I knew the players stretched and cooled off. The game was still going, but since it was spring training, no one cared if players used the foul area as needed.

I just hoped I was stomping in the right direction. My tantrum would lose its impact if I had to turn around and go somewhere else. But Gary said, "down the field," so that was where I was going.

Since being close to the field intimidated me, I stayed close to the wall, where the fans sat. But being close to the fans wasn't any better.

"*Who the hell are you?*" someone shouted.

"*Get off the field, you ugly troll!*" someone else yelled.

"*Booooo, bitch girl!*" Another one said.

It didn't go unnoticed that they were all female voices. I shook my head slightly at their unwarranted disdain, but kept walking. It wasn't the time to try and figure out why women spoke to one another like that.

After a few more steps, I heard the voices again, but that time they were upbeat, happy, and not directed at me.

"Chase!"

"Can I get a pic?"

"Chase, over here!"

I didn't dare look back but I assumed Chase was behind me, which he damn well better have been. When I reached the end of the foul line, I stopped, turned, and placed impatient hands on my hips. Chase had stopped and obliged the fans with a few autographs and pictures and I didn't mind waiting for that—that was what spring training was all about. But those girls were glaring at me like they won a competition that I didn't know we were in.

Meanwhile, I was just glad Chase seemed to be heeding my warning about tearing his balls off and followed me out. It was going to make dealing with Gary that much easier.

"Gotta go before Lady Goliath down there tears me apart," Chase pointed toward me.

Lady Goliath.

He said it with reverence and without an ounce of malice. Like I was in charge and he respected me for it. It felt way better than Princess. I swear I wanted to kick his ass and be his best friend, all at the same time.

"Damn, Cupcake," he whispered as he got closer. "You did better than I thought you would, with the whole balls comment and all."

"Excuse me?"

"What?"

"What do you mean, I did better than you thought I would? Were you expecting my tirade?"

"From the time I came in the dugout and asked Gary to get you, yes, I absolutely was."

"You asked for me? Why the hell did you give me so much shit, then?" I raised my voice a little too loud and almost forgot there were fans, cameras, and people everywhere. It wasn't the time and especially not the place to have a Chase-induced meltdown.

"Calm down, I thought it may be fun to have someone to hang with while I stretched. And, this shows Gary I'm getting your assistance. And," he held up a finger to stop me from talking so he could finish, "you just used your anger with me to show every single guy in that dugout not to fuck with you. It's a win-win-win."

"You have got to be kidding me," I groaned, while still fighting a smile. "Are you even feeling tightness?"

"Um, no. I lied."

"Of course, you did…" I trailed off as Chase sat down in the grass. He started the routine I had taught him that morning to help his knees, then, I also reminded him to do his glutes, quads, and core.

"Get my hand," he said, angling his body away from me and bringing his arm toward me. I took his hand and pulled, earning a groan from deep in his throat. Then we went to the other side, making the same groan fall from his mouth. It was heated—down deep and full of pleasure and I had to stand up to shake off the flush it had given me.

"Jog up the line and back then I think you're good until tonight," I suggested. Without even arguing, he did as I said and finished up. When he was all done, we started making our way back to the dugout together.

A few fans yelled again, but nothing too bad. Chase ignored them that time and walked side by side with me. Somehow, having his attention gave me a sense of relief. I felt smug knowing the girls that were yelling at me were not getting his attention. I even gave a loud laugh at *nothing*. Chase looked at me, confused, surely wondering what I was laughing at, but I just waved him off.

It wasn't like me to be petty. I was a 'women should empower women' kind of girl. But fuck them for being nasty toward me simply because I had a job.

Once we were through the dugout and down the hall, I made

Chase stop so we could be alone before going into the locker room. "I have to get with the other guys, but you need to meet me tonight at seven. We will work on the machines and rub some stuff on your knees."

"Yes ma'am," he saluted and smiled. "I'll bring dinner, Princess."

chase

Day one of the '*Becca and Chase Pact*' was officially underway.

To be fair, I shouldn't have had her come to the field on the first day of games with a crowd around us. But I couldn't resist, and even though she threatened to rip my balls off, she handled it well.

After resting at the hotel for a bit, I grabbed us some dinner and made my way back to the stadium. She was already there–probably hadn't left–and a small part of me felt guilty for making her stay late and help me every night. The other part of me rubbed my hands together in evil satisfaction. Selfishly, I wanted her wherever I had to be.

But I tried to make it as easy on her as possible. Which was why I was carrying six different meals I had the hotel prepare and wrap up to go. Without knowing what she liked, I just got a variety.

When I approached the doors to the training room, I used my foot to gently push the swinging door open. Becca had her back to me, dressed in a sports bra and the smallest pair of shorts I had ever seen. She had one arm bent over the top of her head and was leaning to the side in a stretching motion. Since she didn't know I was there yet, I bit my lip to keep myself from groaning, and took her in.

Her long, dark blonde hair was pulled into a messy ponytail, and her skin looked flush like she had been sweating. I could have stood there all night like a creep, but when I adjusted the bags of food, the rustling noise made her jump around.

"Shit, you scared me."

"Sorry." I tried to act like I had just walked in to keep her from busting on me about lurking.

As she made her way to the table, she grabbed a t-shirt from a bag and pulled it over her head. "I just got done with my own workout," she sighed in frustration. "It's the only time I can squeeze in any self-care."

"I brought dinner, though."

The bite in her features softened a little. "Thanks, I'm starving."

"Look, I know this isn't ideal, but I'll try and make it as easy as possible."

"Like calling me onto the field and subjecting me to nasty fangirl remarks on the first damn day?"

Wait, what? "What do you mean?"

"Those girls you were taking pics with, they were downright nasty with me when I was walking out there alone. That's why I laughed on the way back to the dugout. They were less bitchy when you were next to me. Not wanting to show you their true colors, I guess."

"Oh shit, I didn't even realize that. What did they say?"

She waved me off and let it go. "Nothing. It isn't worth my ire. I'm just so tired. It's been a long day and it's been on my mind."

Those girls were regulars, so even though I was letting it go the way Becca suggested, I wasn't going to forget. I'd protect her from any catty remarks from there on out. No one was going to make her crazy except me. That was my job.

With the dim lights, there wasn't a good place to eat, but I improvised and pulled my phone out, turning on the flashlight. Laying it facing up, it created a glow between us, almost like candlelight, and I began putting the spread of food out.

"Thanks for this." Becca was softening more and more as she took bites from each plate I had brought. "Don't eat too much, though. You're about to do twenty minutes on the treadmill in there."

"Yes ma'am," I smirked then winked, making her slightly flush. "So, tell me about yourself."

"Is this a date?"

"No," I scoffed. *Maybe.* "I just thought since we are spending so much time together, maybe we should get to know each other."

She searched my eyes for my true intent before finally answering me. "Okay then. I'm twenty-seven, an only child, parents died, no friends, studied at Washington State, live in Marietta, and am obsessed with carrot cake."

She was lying to me.

I wasn't sure how I knew, but I knew. So I decided to play her game. "Hmmm, well I'm twenty-nine, have six brothers and sisters, parents are still married, went to Oklahoma University, live in Atlanta, and I'm obsessed with chocolate donuts."

"Lies," she mumbled, taking another bite.

"Yeah? How you figure?"

"Because Google told me you were thirty-three, an only child, mom passed away a few years ago, you went to Auburn University, and, well, you probably live in Atlanta and love donuts."

My mouth dropped open in disbelief. Not because she was right, but because she'd Googled me, and that put me at a disadvantage. Yet, I loved that she'd Googled me.

"I call bullshit on you, too."

"Yeah? How you figure?" She repeated my exact question.

"Your eyes aren't dark enough to have lost your parents. They're not lonely enough to have spent a lifetime alone, either.

Which means you have friends, or siblings, keeping you company. You could have studied in Washington, and you may live in Marietta, probably even love carrot cake, but I'm not wrong about the first two."

She forced a smile and took another bite before speaking again. "I'm twenty-seven, one younger brother and two older sisters. Parents are alive and well. I studied in Athens, and live in Marietta. And yes, I love carrot cake."

I didn't respond, but my eyes were asking her why she suddenly got honest.

"Just thought I would even the playing field," she said. "It's not fair that I can Google you."

"I'm kind of glad I was worth Googling."

"Eh," she shrugged with a small smile. "I was curious."

The rest of the meal was silent, but it wasn't awkward. It was comfortable and peaceful. We were content on being in each other's company.

After we finished, we went into the room on the other side of the glass windows, where the equipment was. As promised, she started me on the treadmill and then moved me to a leg-lifting machine. My knees screamed, but she assured me I had to endure the pain to strengthen them.

Once that was done, she rubbed an icy-hot ointment on me and wrapped gauze around them to hold in the burn. Then we shared a ride back to the hotel, and the night was over.

But I didn't sleep. Not even a wink.

I took a cold shower, tried to think of something that wasn't her, and watched every late show I could find. When that was done, I played on my phone, Googled myself, and listened to music, trying everything to get sleepy.

But the only thing I could do was think of Becca in those shorts.

The sweat around her hairline.

The flush of her skin.

Her toned legs.

Her deep eyes.

Fuck it.

Shoving my hand below my waistband, I grabbed my dick and let that image fuel my lust. It had been a while since I jerked my own cock, but there was no way I'd get through the days with her without some sort of release.

The other option was to head downstairs to the hotel bar, grab anyone that looked my way, and use them for a few hours in my bed. But that didn't feel right. Not when Becca's body was the only image I could manage. Not when she was the one causing me to feel so uncontrollably aroused.

With my hand holding tight, I thrust my hips up and envisioned Becca over top of me, begging me to push harder into her core. Her hands on my chest, her knees spread on either side of my waist, her head thrown back in pleasure.

Even a fantasy with her and my hand was better than any pussy I had ever had. Becca was ruining me without even trying.

The next few days were the same. Early mornings, four innings of baseball, Becca on the field with me, and late nights in the training room gym. I brought dinner, and we always ate under the light of my phone's flashlight. Then when I got back to my room, I'd fuck my own hand to the image of her on top of me.

As the days passed, it seemed like soft lighting in the training room and as we ate, got more and more intimate. At first, I thought it was just because I was getting off to fantasies of her every night. But then, our conversations got more intimate as well. I didn't dare tell her about my dad, but I did talk about my mom and her death—a heart attack. She spoke about her parents a little, and her sisters, though I noticed she steered clear of mentioning her brother.

By the end of the week, we had moved past families and friends, and she asked me something I didn't want to talk about—nor did I want to lie about it either.

"What makes this year so special? Why not just fess up to the knee issues and fix them? I don't get it."

Of course, she didn't, because I barely did.

I knew I let myself down in the offseason. I didn't condition the way I should have. I had something to prove to myself. I also knew I didn't have to deal with my dad as long as I played. I knew that baseball was my life, and my playing days were numbered as I got older. I wanted to soak up as much of it as I could.

None of that was something I wanted to admit to her, though. Those were my weaknesses, and I didn't want her to think I was weak. So I gave her the only truth I could think of.

"One hundred and twenty million," I smiled and locked eyes with her.

"Dollars?" she gasped.

"Yep," I nodded. "That is how much I'm worth after this season if I stay healthy and on my game."

"Holy shit," she said in awe. "You must like money."

Ouch!

"I like the respect that comes along with it, that's for damn sure." Another truth.

"I see." She wiped her lips with a napkin and threw it on her to-go box. "Let's get to work then."

"What? Not going to give me shit for how much I *love* money?"

"I'm not going to give you shit for how much you crave respect. That I can relate to."

"Touché," I replied as I stood and got ready for the workout. It had only been a week, but I was progressing where my knees were concerned. There was pain, but Becca made it possible to power through during games, and I just hoped as I played more and more, I'd be able to handle it.

What I couldn't handle was the way Becca kept looking at me, like she was a lion and I was her lamb. For the first time since we met, I no longer felt like the one out of control. She was antsy and fidgeting, but her eyes were unwavering as I jogged on the treadmill.

"Stop, Princess," I warned.

"Stop what?" Her lips were moving, but her eyes stayed in place.

"Stop looking at my dick."

"I wasn't looking at your… thing…" She turned a bright shade of red and her eyes came to mine, as if she was trying to prove that she wasn't looking at the way my cock bounced between my legs.

"Yes, you were."

"Well shit, Chase, it's just there, and big, and shit."

I nearly fell off the treadmill as I stutter-stepped at her words so I brought my arms to the handles to brace myself in case I fell. Then I lowered the speed to a casual pace so I could think.

"Didn't you give me some speech the other day about how we were only human?" She started in on me.

There was no way I was going to be able to keep going, so I stopped the treadmill all together and hopped off. "Come on, Cupcake. Let's change the scenery."

She didn't even question me or stall, just jumped from her spot and started grabbing her bag. "Thank God."

"Leave your stuff, come on." Instinctively, I grabbed her hand and laced our fingers together. When she didn't fight my hold, I guided her from the training room to the locker room, and down the hallway toward the dugout.

It was eerily dark and quiet, but I had made that walk a million times in my career, and I could do it with my eyes closed. Becca was quiet, but I could hear her breathing getting sharper, and she squeezed my hand tighter. Whether it was fear or reflex, I wasn't sure, but she wasn't asking any questions.

The light started shining in from the field when we got closer to the dugout. Like everywhere else in the stadium, the lights were set to a timer, and only emergency lights remained on. On the field, there were just enough lights to see but not enough to keep from seeing the stars.

"Is this okay?" Becca finally asked in a whisper.

"I don't see why not."

"I don't want to get in trouble, Chase."

"Princess, I would never do anything to get you in trouble."

I couldn't see her well, but I knew she rolled her eyes at me. "Tell that to your bouncing thing."

The laugh I barked out was loud and echoed down the tunnel. But her attempt at avoiding the word "dick" or "cock" only made her more endearing.

"How in the hell would that get you in trouble?" I asked, but I already knew. We were both at a point where we were tiptoeing an imaginary line that we didn't dare cross. It was out there, between us, that we found each other tempting. But that would definitely be trouble.

She didn't even humor me with an answer.

As we emerged from the dugout, her breath caught a little, and she squeezed my hand again. The field was different at night when it was quiet and empty. There was something celestial about it. It held beauty and mystery all at the same time.

"What are we doing out here?"

"Just thought it would be a good place to finish my stretches." Reluctantly, I dropped her hand and walked to the grass between the pitcher's mound and home plate. When I was halfway there, I turned and walked backward, imploring her to follow me.

Her eyes stayed on my face but she took steps, getting closer. When she got within range, I grabbed her hand again and sat down, encouraging her to sit with me. She knelt between the V in my legs, putting us eye level with one another.

I couldn't move, selfishly wishing she would throw caution to the wind and kiss me. It had to be her decision because she had more to lose. That wasn't something I could take away from her.

Maybe it wasn't a good idea to go out to the field, because it was making it more complicated. Like one bad decision could easily lead us to the next. One of us had to move, but I could only halfway convince myself to break the spell.

Pushing her onto her back, I laid beside her and kept her hand in mine. Below the stars, in the soft grass, we laid side by side, looking up, without hands still locked together.

"Thank you," she whispered.

It took me a minute, but I realized she was thanking me for breaking the spell. For being the one who was strong enough to change our view.

"I'm putting you through enough shit, Princess. I won't add one more thing."

She didn't respond, just kept staring at the stars above. Five minutes passed before she finally spoke again—so low I could barely hear her.

"I think you already have."

becca

A FEW DAYS LATER, CHASE AND I WERE STILL TIPTOEING AROUND our mutual attraction to one another. Since the night we laid together under the stars, things had gotten both better and worse.

Better, because Chase had become a manageable human. He was diligent with the workouts and didn't give me nearly as much trouble as he had been. He had also stopped calling me Princess, Cupcake, or any other made-up name he concocted.

Worse, because I kind of missed the shit he gave me. I missed the nicknames and the things he would say that made me roll my eyes into the back of my head.

His demeanor was stoic and professional.

Our dinners were silent.

Our workouts were nothing more than grunts.

Our conversations were clipped.

But when he gave me tiny pockets of himself, small windows of the good-natured, shit-giving, caring-as-hell Chase, I swooned even harder than before. I relished those moments when he gave me that original version of himself.

He would grumble incoherently in the mornings, making it

awkward and miserable. But then he would point to where he had my favorite coffee delivered to his room before I got there. One night, a carrot cake was delivered to my room without a note or anything, but I knew it was him.

Small gestures.

It didn't take a genius to realize he was emotionally distancing himself to mitigate the fire that grew around us. And while I understood and appreciated the effort, it wasn't working—at all.

While he was on the field playing his fifth inning of the day, I was in the locker room with Manny. Manny hated me, but since his x-rays had indeed shown inflammation, he gave me a little respect.

In my opinion, I didn't deserve his respect, but I was going to take it. After all, if it wasn't for my little white lie, he wouldn't have been playing much longer anyway. And after not playing for almost a week, he was getting ready to replace Chase in the game/

"Two innings today," I told him as I wrapped his knee. "Then we'll make sure the fluid doesn't build again. If it doesn't, three innings tomorrow, and so on."

"Yep," he said before hopping off the table and walking toward the dugout.

As he walked out, Troy walked in and said my five least favorite words during a game. "Gary is asking for you."

Looking toward the TV, I saw that the Kings were still on the field, which meant Chase hadn't come in yet. Plus, he had one more inning to play.

When I got to the dugout and sat beside Gary, I expected him to tell me someone besides Chase needed me. But as I approached to where he was leaning on the rail, he didn't even look my way, keeping his eyes on the field.

"Does he look funny to you?" he pointing, guiding my eyes toward Chase.

Chase was kneeling behind the plate. From my angle, I could

see his profile behind his mask and only his right hand and right knee. He had beads of sweat dripping down the side of his face, and his left hand was gloved and held out, waiting for the next pitch.

Everything seemed fine, at first. Then, I noticed what Gary was referring to. As the pitch came toward him, Chase took his right hand and squeezed his knee. Once he caught the ball, he threw it back and grabbed his knee once again.

"Yeah, I would say there may be a problem." *Uh oh. Were we busted?*

Without acknowledging that he heard me, Gary shouted to the coach, "I need to check on Turner."

The coach nodded and emerged from the dugout, asking for a timeout. Gary started walking toward the entrance to the dugout, and I looked on to see how it would all play out.

Unfortunately, Gary had different plans.

"Get out here, Becca. I want you with me."

Interns didn't do that, so I assumed he was lying. Why on earth would he need me out there? But one more look from Gary and I scrambled to catch up to him.

All the infielders, the coach, and an umpire were on the pitcher's mound, waiting on us as we walked out. Chase's eyes—and Kace's—were wider than saucers, watching me approach with Gary.

Straightening my shoulders, I was determined to be poised in the incredibly unusual situation. All I had to do was nod and listen, take in anything I learned by being out there with my boss.

But then Gary turned to me and motioned for me to talk.

Seriously, Gary?

Chase and I were barely talking to each other off the field. And he wanted me to have a chat out there in the middle of what felt like the entire world? Panic was about to set in.

"Um," I looked at Chase so he knew I was talking to him and cleared my throat. "Why are you grabbing your knee?"

Did I sound like an idiot? *Probably.*

Switching from one foot to the other, I impatiently waited for his response. When Chase looked to Gary without answering, though, I let my panic go a little and toughened up.

"What's up with your knee?" I repeated, getting his attention back on me before he could speak to Gary.

"Nothing. A bruise."

Gary looked at me again and I knew I had to make a decision and make it quick. We were in the middle of the field. The other team was waiting. The fans were waiting.

And I was about to blow their minds.

On the surface and in their minds, Chase was always honest and probably just had a boo-boo. But I knew he had underlying knee issues–and lying issues–and I felt compelled to get him off the field as soon as possible just in case it was more than a bruise.

Gary would probably disagree with me, and Chase definitely would, but I went with what my gut was telling me to do.

"You should go ahead and come in with me. Call it a day. Manny is ready to play, anyway."

"What?" His eyes narrowed, not quite believing me. Or was he just daring me to repeat myself?

"You were only going to play one more inning. You're obviously in pain. Let's go check it out." My voice was calm and I clapped my hands together as it if wasn't a big deal.

"I'm not leaving this field, Princess."

Oh, so we're back to that, huh?

"Right here? Right now? Really?" I snapped at him. "In front of the world, Butter Boy? Because I don't feel like threatening you with bodily harm right now, but I will."

Chase's lips quirked just a little, so little I would have missed it if I hadn't spent half my time analyzing his stupid, perfect lips. He was amused at my outburst but still determined not to come off that field.

He looked to the coach and Gary, glossing over my threat to

bargain with them. "I'll make you a deal. Two more outs and I'll walk off myself."

"No," I snapped, not giving Chase the satisfaction of going over my head.

Chase started gritting his teeth, warring with himself. And probably mentally warring with me. But I was ready and waiting for his next protest.

Much to the shock of everyone standing there, Chase turned and walked to the dugout, his posture indicating he was beyond pissed. Even though Gary was the one who called me out there, he let me take the lead, and I was going to pay once Chase and I were alone.

Before I turned to follow Chase off the field, I caught a quick glimpse of Kace's expression. He looked proud of me, which empowered me.

Chase and I made our way down the tunnel and directly to the training room. The other interns were idling around, waiting for players to come in from the field. But Chase didn't give them a chance to say anything or even blink before he started yelling.

"Out!"

Oh shit, he wasn't talking to me. He was talking to them, and they weren't moving.

"Out, now!" he yelled louder. That time, they stood quickly and ran out of the door. I started to follow them, thinking maybe I should leave Chase alone and give him a minute. But before I reached the door, he added, "Not you, Princess."

His tone had softened. He wasn't yelling at me like he had with the other guys and it made my head spin with confusion.

"Was that another test?" I asked when we were finally alone. Was he trying to get me to be tough in front of everyone?

"No, Cupcake, it wasn't."

"So, we *are* back to that, I see."

"Back to what?"

"The names!" I practically yelled from frustration and

nervousness. It felt like I was being tested, but if not by Chase, then definitely by Gary, and that was probably worse.

"We were never *not* there," Chase said.

All I could do was sigh in more frustration. I knew it wasn't the time or place to worry about what he called me and I needed to focus more on what we needed to do.

"Three questions for you: Why are you grabbing at your knee when you squat? What made you finally walk off the field a minute ago? And why did you just yell at everyone like a maniac?"

Chase held up his thumb to answer the first question. "One, I took a ball off the kneecap in the first inning. It stung, right up under my shin guards. I guess instinct had me grabbing at it, because I didn't realize I was doing it." He held up his pointer finger for his next point. "Two, I have nothing to prove but you do, and Gary needed to know you've got this. So I came in here and gave you the win." I started to talk, but he cut me off with his third finger going up. "And three, I yelled at them to get out because I'm not about to let them see us together, like this. It's asking for trouble and easier if they think I'm just mad at every-thing. Or a maniac, as you put it."

"Aren't you just mad, though?"

"Not even close, baby," he said softly, leaving it at that—with a new nickname and no explanation.

I tried not to acknowledge how weak I was around him. I was trying to think of something to say, anything other than, *"I love it when you call me baby,"* as I melted into a puddle at his feet.

Luckily, I was saved by a text message and pulled my phone out to check it.

Gary.

Get me a workup on Turner before he leaves the stadium.

Yes, sir.

Looking to Chase, it was if he had read my mind, and he started undoing his chest protector. Keeping his eyes on me, he slipped it over his head, then started unlatching his shin guards. It was like a striptease, with catcher's gear, and way sexier to me than had he just been completely naked.

Once the shin guards were off, he slipped his wrist protector off his left arm—eyes still on me. Then he went to his belt, undid the buckle, and unzipped his pants. I looked down at his calves and realized how tight his pants were tapered. They wouldn't stretch over his knee, so taking his pants down was most likely the best way.

Oh shit. My breathing got harder, borderline hyperventilating, and Chase took note, pausing with his hands on his waistband.

"Relax, I have sliding shorts on," he whispered.

Not that I didn't want to see him naked again, but I was relieved he had sliding shorts on. I was too keyed up to deal with a naked baseball player.

"I have to give Gary something before you leave," I rambled something he already knew.

He nodded as he slid his pants down and jumped onto the table. His cleats were still on, preventing his pants from coming off, and once he was situated, he nodded to the bruise on his knee.

"When did this happen? Specifically."

"Second pitch of the game. A slider that hit the dirt. Got right under the pad and stung. But it's not internal, Cupcake. I promise. I know that's why you made the decision to shut me down."

"I was worried," I nodded. "Gary said something was up with your knee and I thought he knew the truth." I felt around on his knee, being gentle not to apply pressure to the welt darkening under his kneecap. "I'll let Gary know it's just a bruise. But, um, we need to cancel our session tonight. Let this thing rest."

"I still want to see you tonight," he argued.

"You should probably rest your knee—"

"Okay, I will," he cut me off. "But... I still want to see you tonight." Grabbing my hand, he let me know with just a touch that he wasn't talking about professionally. He wanted to see me outside of the office.

And I wanted to see him, too. Especially outside of baseball, and stupid knees. It was a crazy, awful, horrible idea. And I needed to tell him that. But Chase wasn't the idiot I once proclaimed him to be. He knew, without being told, that it was the dumbest idea he had ever had.

It didn't keep him from asking, though. And it sure as hell didn't keep me from replying.

"Okay."

CHAPTER TWELVE
becca

Chase had told me he would pick me up at seven p.m.—our normal meet-up time. He didn't tell me what we were doing, but I prayed he didn't have plans that involved anything fancy because I didn't pack anything cuter than a simple sundress. Which I opted not to wear because it felt too 'date-ish'.

Jeans and a cute top seemed safe.

There was also come confusion with what Chase had meant by *'picking me up.'* We were staying in the same hotel, eight floors apart. It made it impossible to leave together if he really thought he would just drive out front and pick me up. Someone would notice.

When a knock sounded on my door at seven p.m., I paused for a minute, thinking he was crazy that his little plan was going to work. But when I finally opened the door, it wasn't Chase. It was a hotel concierge… with a wheelchair.

The confused look on my face was the only push the man needed to clear his throat and explain. "Hi, Princess?" The words were a question and uncomfortable. He did not want to say it, but he did, and I laughed out loud, wondering how much Chase paid him to do it.

"He had better have paid you well!" I laughed, shaking my head.

"Um, yes ma'am," he motioned to the wheelchair. "And he's asked me to deliver you to the parking garage."

"Why a wheelchair?"

"No idea, ma'am. Something about knees and being funny and me picking you up physically being inappropriate."

"Oh, good God, he's got to be kidding. I can walk."

Closing the door, I started walking down the hall, but the concierge quickly got behind me, pushing the chair.

"Ma'am, he told me you must be in the chair."

"I'm not letting you push me around," I reasoned, and pushed the button for the elevator.

"Ma'am, Mr. Turner was clear. You must be in the chair."

"He isn't that big of an asshole." *Is he?* I didn't know Chase well, but I did know he was very capable of being an asshole. And that poor guy wanted the tip badly enough that he was practically begging me to get in the chair.

"I'm not sure of that, ma'am." He backed off, riding a fine line between working for his tip and pissing off a guest.

Luckily for him, I wasn't an asshole. He was middle-aged and probably just trying to work hard and pay his bills. Then Chase comes along and reels him into his shenanigans. So, I sat down right as the elevator doors opened.

"Thank you, thank you." He rolled me backward into the elevator and hit the button to take us below ground level to the parking garage.

"What's your name?"

"Calvin, ma'am."

"Okay Calvin, next time I'm making you give me half of Chase's money. And we're taking him for triple whatever he offered you this time."

My words were lighthearted, and I got a small laugh out of him. "Yes ma'am."

When the elevator doors reopened, he pushed me into the garage and around a corner, where I saw Chase sitting on the hood of a car. His legs were crossed at the ankles, and he leaned back on his arms a little. He was wearing jeans and a plain grey T-shirt.

I was so annoyed, not only from the wheelchair ride but also that he had gotten his way. The smile on his face when seeing me in the wheelchair made it worth the ride, though. His super sexy, arrogant smile, perfect teeth, gorgeous lips and…

"Hey, Princess! You made it."

"Here I am, signed, sealed, and delivered." I waved my hands as if to say "*ta-da*".

Chase leaned over and handed Calvin an ungodly amount of cash, then thanked him. It made me happy I obliged the ride if, for nothing else, it helped Calvin make his next four rent payments.

When I stood from the chair, it disappeared, along with Calvin.

"What was that all about?"

"I told you I would pick you up. I didn't think us marching out of the building together was a good idea."

"You couldn't have just had me meet you here?"

"This was more fun. Plus, for just five minutes, you got to be the patient, not me."

Another ridiculous Chase moment had me rolling my eyes but enjoying every second.

Motioning to the passenger side of his car, Chase let me around and opened the door. As he walked around the front of the car, his smile faded just a little as he eyed the dents in the driver's side fender.

"Ready?" he asked, back to his happy demeanor when he slid into the car.

"I guess so. Where're we going?"

"It's a surprise."

Biting my bottom lip, I turned my head away, trying to hide how much I was enjoying the idea of our 'date.'

"Glad you're back," I muttered, thinking of how light he seemed compared to the days before.

"Back?"

"Last few days you have been kinda distant. Not talking much."

"Yeah…I tried…I swear I fucking tried…" he trailed off without elaborating. I figured if I stared at him long enough, he would keep talking and tell me why, but he didn't. Instead, he kept his eyes on the road as he navigated out of the garage and onto the streets.

I was tempted to ask him if we were on a date, or to demand he tell me why he wasn't himself the last few days. But then I got distracted.

Majorly distracted.

By his forearms.

I was officially in sexy forearm territory. I had heard about it. I had read about it. But I thought it was a myth. In fact, I had seen Chase's forearms a million times. So why was I just now being distracted by them?

The way his left leg lifted a little as he pushed in the clutch and his forearms flexed as he shifted from fifth to sixth gear had me biting my lip again and suppressing a groan. I would love to blame my incredible lust on a dry spell, or something logical, but Chase was the only one that seemed to ignite wild feelings inside of me. Being away from work, I got to relax and just be *Becca* around him. And Becca loved looking at Chase's forearms.

After a thirty-minute ride spent having small talk and staring at forearms, the car slowed down, pulling me from my thoughts.

"Disney World?" I looked around in disbelief.

"I know what you're thinking. I shouldn't be walking around Disney World on this knee. But, let me just say, I have arranged everything to keep me off this knee as much as possible."

"That is not what I was thinking. I was thinking, 'Holy shit, Chase, we're at Disney World.' Don't they close soon? It's like eight pm."

"They close at eleven, but we have the park until midnight."

"Oh my God," I muttered as we pulled up right in front of the gate. A valet, wearing Mickey's ears, opened my door, and I met Chase on the sidewalk as the car pulled away.

Another man in a suit–no Mickey ears–stuck his hand out for Chase to shake as he explained our arrangements. "Mr. Turner, we have a cart and driver waiting for you. Here are your passes. Please let us know any way we can make your evening more enjoyable, sir."

"Thank you. I think we're going to be okay."

"Yes sir. Welcome to the Magic Kingdom. Enjoy your visit." He started to turn but then stopped and tilted his head. "And, sir? Everything else has been arranged as well," he added vaguely.

Chase just nodded and grabbed my hand, not bothering to explain.

Using my free hand, I grabbed onto Chase's sexy forearm and squeezed. "This is too much. What are we doing at Disney World?"

"I love Disney World," Chase just shrugged. "I come every year. And I figured it would be a good place to see your friends."

"My friends?" I started panicking a little. Did he know? Ali and Cam were supposed to come and see Kace next week. What if they were there at Disney?

"You know," Chase finally elaborated. "Snow White, Aurora, Belle, Ariel, all those other princesses."

Princess.

I couldn't help but giggle at not only his logic, but in relief.

"What if someone recognizes you and sees us together?"

"Nobody will recognize me."

"How can you be sure?"

"I can't be sure, but we'll do our best to be discreet."

As we entered the back gate, there was a golf cart covered in Mickey silhouettes and a driver dressed as Goofy waiting for us.

"This is your idea of being discreet?"

"It's Disney World, no one questions Goofy driving a red and black golf cart, trust me," he shrugged.

Disney World was a terrible idea, but it was already established that Chase and I didn't shy away from terrible ideas. We were practically pros at that point. What was one more bad idea?

We climbed onto the cart and were driven all over the park, Goofy as our guide. We saw everything there was to see and stopped and rode a few rides along the way, skipping straight to the front of the lines.

We grabbed dole whips and giant pretzels to snack on, laughed until our stomachs hurt, and snapped selfies together. Other than holding hands, everything was platonic and friendly, making it easier to relax and have fun.

By the time eleven p.m. came, I was high on Disney and high on Chase Turner. The night couldn't have been any more perfect. Especially after the crowd diminished to just those that held late-night passes, and we decided to walk around a bit, leaving Goofy and our cart to follow us a safe distance behind.

"This was incredible, Chase."

"You haven't even seen the best part," he winked.

Looking up at him as we strolled down Main Street, USA., I smiled. "What's the best part?"

Was he going to kiss me? I secretly hoped the best part was would be another terrible idea.

Chase intertwined his fingers with mine and lifted them to point to a building ahead. "We gotta go in there."

The building looked like an old general store, but nothing could be seen through the windows. Chase smiled at a guard at the gate and walked past, opening the door and escorting me in.

Just inside the doorway, I paused and gasped, making Chase bump into me from behind as he tried following me in. His hands made their way to my waist and he grabbed me tight. It was the most intimate he had ever touched me, and I almost lost focus on what was in front of me.

Almost.

"Go in, Princess," he whispered in my ear, pushing at my hips to get me to move.

"Chase…" I warned, on the edge of an epic girl moment that could possibly scare him.

He just laughed a little, enjoying my response.

"Chase..." I warned again.

"It's like a reunion," he whispered into my ear again, humor lacing his words.

Every Disney princess ever created stood before me, poised and lined up in formation. The leading twelve princesses were in front, along with Elsa and Anna. They weren't statues but people who portrayed those characters every day. They were the real-life versions of every girl's princess dreams.

"Welcome," Belle spoke first and curtsied in front of me.

"We wanted to meet you, Princess Becca," Anna added.

Their voices were in character, and my seven-year-old self practically jumped for joy. Elsa held her arms out, coaxing me to join them so I walked forward and was asked by a woman with a camera to turn around and smile for a picture.

Right in the middle, I turned and posed, looking beyond the camera at Chase. He had the most infectious smile and he needed to be in one of the pictures. His smile needed to be seen, so I waved for him to join me.

"Not a good idea, Cupcake."

"First of all, I am a princess, not a cupcake," I teased. "Second of all, no one has to see it but us. When are you ever going to be surrounded by this many princesses again?"

He looked down, a slight pink in his cheeks as he started walking toward us. He stood for a few pictures, mostly us together, but I insisted that he get one with him alone, surrounded by royalty and looking like the king of the world.

My family had been to Disney a countless number of times, but not once had I seen every princess together in one place. Chase had gone to a lot of trouble to make it happen and I didn't think I would ever understand why. All I knew was that I think I loved him for it.

chase

SOMEHOW, I MADE IT ALL NIGHT WITHOUT SUCCUMBING TO THE temptation to kiss Becca. She wanted me to. She wouldn't have turned me away.

But I couldn't do it.

I knew the second our lips touched that it would forever change the paths we were creating for ourselves. Our careers were our priority, and before we threw it all away, we needed more time to figure out what was happening between us.

For a few days, I had tried to play it cool and not talk as much to her so I could keep some emotional distance. But then I would be sitting in my hotel room and think, *"I bet she would love a carrot cake,"* and then end up sending one to her room. It was probably a mindfuck, but I tried.

Admittedly, taking her to Disney World was over the top, but I couldn't think of anything more memorable for what would probably be our only night out together. Making her smile was my only goal, but it ended up being so much more. The whole experience softened us. She was looking at me differently. She was smiling more easily. She was giggling.

Becca was beautiful every time I saw her, but she was downright addicting when she was happy and free. I wanted more of that freedom, more of her happiness. And I wanted it to be because of me.

During the day, at work, she was stoic and strong, working tirelessly. Then in the evening, she lowered her walls and gave me a side to her that only I got to see. It would have been so much easier if she were anyone else, working anywhere else. It would be simpler if I didn't really care, and chose to take whatever I wanted.

But I more than cared about her. I wanted to see her succeed and would never forgive myself if I was the reason she couldn't retain her job with the Kings.

So I didn't fucking kiss her.

Not at Disney, not when I dropped her off, and not the next morning when she knocked on my door for out warmups. She came to my door like always, and I handed her a coffee, not gruffing and groaning the way I had the days before. I was staying resolute to ruin her career, but I didn't have it in me to avoid her and not talk to her anymore.

Especially when she walked in with a smile and wrapped her arms around my midsection. She pressed her cheek into my t-shirt-covered chest and I wrapped my arms around her in what may have been the best hug of my life.

"What's this for?"

She pulled back slightly, just enough to look up at me, her chin now on my chest. "Last night was the best night I've had in a long time. Who did you have to sweet talk to get all the princesses in one room?"

"Maybe it was the magic of Disney," I joked and swallowed hard, thinking of how easy it would be to press my lips to hers from that angle.

"Maybe. But whoever arranged the magic must have gone through a lot of trouble."

"Maybe it was worth it."

We stared at each other for a minute, the spell between us more potent than ever. When I finally backed away, I cleared my throat to break the tension, and we got to work on our regular routines. The swelling on my knee had barely gone down, but I told her I still didn't regret Disney, even if that meant I had to sit the next game out.

Which that though alone blew my mind more than she would ever know, because I meant it. I wouldn't change taking her to Disney for anything—not even baseball.

Fuck! Was I screwed?

There was no way I was going to be able to keep backing off when it came to Becca. Eventually, I was going to break and take her down in the process. So I either needed to warn her, or have a nice long chat with myself about all the bad ideas I kept coming up with.

First, though, I had to play ball.

Coach decided I would put three innings on my bruised knee, and Gary agreed I would work out after those three innings were done. When he sent Troy to get Becca, I knew we were headed down the field to stretch like we did before—the day she got hassled by a few fans.

Those same fans, I noticed, were in the stands again. So I didn't give Becca the same shit I had before. I just nodded that I would meet her out there and she nodded back, solemnly preparing herself for her walk past the fans.

Fans came in there all the time, spewing hatred and abhorrence. That was the nature of the business. If I kicked everyone out that said something ugly, we would have empty stands every day. But that didn't mean I couldn't be her hero.

Letting Becca walk ahead a bit, I listened, and when they started calling her a *bitch* and a baseball bunny—whatever the fuck that was–it took all my strength to not make a scene.

Becca had kept her head down, trying to ignore them, but I knew she heard. I knew she was affected. Grabbing Ethan and our starting centerfielder, Kris, I told them what was happening and without even hesitating, they jogged out with me and together, we surrounded Becca. Our presence made her stop walking, but it also made the fans stop yelling. Their attention had turned to the players, but none of us gave them a glance.

With Kris to her right, Ethan to her left, and me standing directly behind her, we had created a defensive wall to make her feel secure and special. Placing a hand discreetly on Becca's back, I urged her to keep walking while Kris leaned in and whispered something to her. Ethan grabbed her shoulders and pretended to steer her around playfully, making her laugh.

We all cared about Becca and our level of petty had nothing to do with how I was feeling for her. Just like when Fernandez called her a bitch, we rallied around her and took care of her as if she was a teammate.

Once we made our way downfield, Ethan hung out for a minute joked around, laughing while I started my stretches. Kris grabbed a glove and started tossing a ball back and forth with a kid in the stands. If Becca knew why we were all out there, she didn't let on. She just went about her business as usual. Ethan even told her about a blister he didn't think was getting taken care of properly, and she advised him on what to do.

Eventually, Kris got called back to the dugout, and Ethan went into the bullpen to help another pitcher who had been struggling. Becca and I were alone as I finished up, jogging down the line a few times.

"Wanna hang with me while I sign some autographs?" I asked, already knowing her answer would be no. Despite there being a few bad seeds, spring training was about fans, and I always tried to sign a few autographs when I wrapped up my day.

"No, Pancake, you can handle that on your own. And I can manage my walk back to the dugout without my protection team."

Busted.

"I have no regrets," I laughed.

"Well I'm sure you guys sent a message, loud and clear. I'll be fine."

"You sure? I can arrange a new escort," I half-joked, not wanting anyone else to be her hero but not wanting her to be alone, either.

"Positive."

Giving her a quick wink, I headed to the side rail to see some small kids asking for a picture. From the corner of my eye, though, I kept an eye on her. She had her clipboard up and a pen, jotting down notes. She was always writing and walking, but that time felt somewhat strategic. Staying busy to keep her mind off and look busy as she made her way past the fans.

But it didn't stop the comments. I could hear them start yelling again the second Becca got close enough. The word *"whore"* was yelled loudly and I started making my way toward her, just as a baseball was thrown onto the field, hitting Becca hard in the side of the head.

Maybe they had good aim and hit the target, or perhaps they were just trying to scare her and it was an accident. Either way, it caused Becca to fall and I raced toward her, beating everyone else that had come to help, including Gary. The game had been halted, security was hauling the fans away, and I had to be pulled away by my teammates so the medical staff could check on her properly.

Guilt raced through me as I wondered if I had caused them to escalate their hatred. Ignoring them and putting Becca first may have been what caused her to be hurt. Ethan caught up to me and somehow knew I was blaming myself, because he tapped my back and tried to console me.

"Having her back and protecting her was never the wrong move."

Once Becca was standing again, I tried to sidle up next to her, but couldn't get through the crowd of people around her. She began shoving everyone away, telling them she was fine, and they tried to give her space. But when she took a stutter step, everyone crowded in again.

Including Kace Jackson.

Why was he there?

He had come in, all the way from shortstop and was pushing everyone away from her. He even grabbed her shoulders, trying to console her. I had no doubt that he didn't want her being attacked any more than the rest of us, but somehow, his reaction felt personal.

The only thing that kept my brain from wandering too far down that track was that she pushed him away like she did the others. When I tried, though, she leaned into me, and I took her hand to guide her to the dugout. She didn't fight, or say she was okay, just held on tightly as we walked, and I assured her that she was okay and safe.

Taking her through the tunnel, the locker room, and into Gary's office, I sat with her on the couch with both of my arms wrapped around her, holding her to my chest. Gary was the only one with us, and I just hoped he didn't read too much into how protective I felt over Becca.

"I got it from here, Turner," Gary grumbled.

Looking up at him, I was ready to tell him to fuck off, but I silently repeated to myself that I wasn't supposed to be attached to Becca. Nor was I supposed to care, or be too concerned. My part was loaning her a helping hand like a good human, and I was supposed to get lost once she was safe.

But I couldn't do that. She was *my* Becca. I couldn't leave her.

"This is my fault," I tried to explain, hoping it would show him why I wasn't leaving.

"How?"

Should I tell him the truth? Or lie?

"She wouldn't have been out there if I didn't need her," I reasoned.

"That's ridiculous," Gary replied.

"Gary is right," Becca finally whispered. "This isn't your fault, Chase. I would have been out there no matter who needed me. It's my job."

Becca wanted me to leave it at that, to not make it a big deal. As far as Gary was concerned, it was a case of being in the wrong place at the wrong time.

When Gary turned away and started rummaging through a cabinet, I locked eyes with Becca and she mouthed, "I'm okay."

Even though I was guilt-ridden and sad, and wasn't ready to leave her, she wanted me to go. She needed me to go. One last peek at Gary, to make sure he was still distracted, and I took my lips to the swelling on the side of her forehead. My kiss was quiet and soft, and wouldn't technically heal her, but I wanted to pretend it would. At the very least, I hope it showed her how sorry I was.

"Okay, well, hope you feel better," I stood, speaking loud enough for Gary to hear me and making a show of casually leaving. "See ya."

"Later," Gary called over his shoulder.

Becca leaned back on the couch and closed her eyes as Gary took an ice pack to her. I closed the door and walked to the locker room, done for the day, and knowing I could head back to the hotel. But leaving, knowing Becca was still in there, didn't sit well with me.

Plus, I had something I needed to figure out.

chase

"Hey Kace," I hollered across the locker room as I entered. He was just coming off the field and out of the game for the day.

"Hey, can't talk right now." He was in a hurry and looked frantic, grabbing his phone from his locker, not paying me any mind.

"I just have a quick question." Actually, I had a lot of questions. They all centered around why the fuck he ran all the way in from shortstop to see about Becca.

There were players everywhere, and a part of me thought I may have been overreacting. But he was the only one who looked like he was in physical pain. He didn't just run to her, he left his position on the field.

"Not her."

"Trust me."

His words from the first day I saw Becca came back to me. Before the rest of us, he knew that Becca was off-limits. How?

Before I could ask him about it, he was gone—full uniform, cleats, and dirt—ignoring my request to ask him anything. So I just went back to my room and sat there, staring at a blank TV and hoping Becca would text me, call me, send smoke signals.

Anything.

Something.

She never did, though, and by ten p.m., I decided to head to her room, with carrot cake, and check on her. As I exited the elevator on her floor, and began turning toward her door, I saw the back of Kace's head walking down the hall. His room was across from mine, on the twelfth floor. He had as much business being on the fourth floor as I did.

Backing off a bit, I hid behind one of the giant columns in the hallway between each set of doors. I felt like a goddamn kid spying, but my curiosity was bigger than caring about my immaturity level.

Kace stopped at Becca's door and knocked. After a minute, when she still didn't answer, he knocked again.

"Becs, it's me. Open up."

Becs? It's me? He said that like he knew her personally.

"What the fuck are you doing here?" She hissed, as her door flew open.

"Relax, no one saw me, and no one knows I'm here."

"Go away," she demanded.

Was he an ex?

Should I step in and help her?

"You know I can't do that, Becs, let me in." Kace didn't sound urgent or mad. He almost sounded tired. Bored.

"For fuck's sake," she sighed and moved so he could enter.

Once the door was shut, I was left alone in the hallway, completely in shock. Becca never mentioned knowing Kace, but after what I just saw, it was apparent that they knew one another very well.

Becs.

As I walked back down to my room, I asked myself why I cared. But the reason was obvious. I was into Becca. I wanted Becca. She had a lot to lose by having a relationship with a player. If she was going to risk her career, I wanted to be the one she risked it with. And I had been doing my damnedest to respect that while navigating those feelings.

Okay, I was pissed. All that time, I had been mindful of her relationship with me, and she had a relationship, of some sort, with Kace.

When I returned to my room, I threw the cake, making a mess all over the balcony door. I paced the room and ran my hand through my hair seven hundred times, trying to think about what I had missed. There had to be something else.

But what?

After a few paces, it hit me. The missing piece. The one thing that made the entire situation even stranger. The reason there was no way Kace and Becca were seeing each other romantically.

Kace was in a relationship with Ali Hansen. He shared her with his best friend, Cam Nichols, but he loved her. There was no way he would cheat on her, or end things. I had never seen a man so committed to someone.

But maybe I was wrong.

becca

It had been the worst day I had ever had on the job. That morning, I woke up thinking it would be the best day, and after the night I had with Chase, how could it not be?

Then reality hit me in the side of the head with a baseball. It was like a reminder that I needed to get my head on straight before Chase and I leapt over the lines we had drawn between one another.

A warning I should have heeded.

Since the game was not televised, Cam only knew about the incident once Kace called him. But I didn't want their attention or concern. I knew they were freaking out, but I hid in Gary's office resting and finishing paperwork. By the time I got back to my room, I had thirty missed calls on my phone between Cam, Ali, and my mom. I knew I should call them back and tell them I was okay, but Kace had to have known I was fine and he could have delivered that message as well.

Meanwhile, all I really wanted was Chase. He had been terrified, almost sick to his stomach, and he hadn't wanted to leave my side. He only did so because he knew he had to, and with it being over, I wanted not only to thank him, but show him I was fine.

However, finding Chase was impossible until I got Kace and Cam off my back. Reluctantly, I texted Cam when I got to my room. Instead of accepting that I was okay, he threatened to fly in unless I let Kace around me long enough to see for himself that I was fine. Which made me roll my eyes so many times I couldn't see straight.

Kace arrived at my door at ten p.m. and I had to think really hard about whether I was going to let him in or not. He and Cam were overprotective, and it got annoying, but they meant well.

"Kace, I swear if anyone saw you come in here, I will slice your fingers off."

"No one saw me, Becs. But you and I both know Cam, and Ali for that matter, are freaking out. Let's just Facetime them together really quickly."

He dialed up Cam as I huffed in annoyance. Cam answered on the first ring and Kace immediately turned the camera towards me.

"Fuck that is going to leave a knot," Cam sighed. "Are you sure you didn't get a concussion?"

"I had one of the best athletic directors checking me out, Cam. I trust his judgement."

"What would have possessed a fan to throw something at you?"

"Honestly, Cam, I think it was just random," I lied. Telling him I was targeted for my gender and role with the team wasn't happening. Telling him Chase, Ethan, and Kris may have caused the woman to go off the rails wasn't going to happen either.

"Cam and I are flying in to see Kace next week, Becca," Ali interjected. "You going to hang with us?"

"I would like that," I said, thankful she changed the subject. "Just not at the stadium. Remember? I don't know you."

"How about dinner downtown after the game one night?"

"Yes!" I was excited to see her. "I usually finish up around 7:30."

"Why so late?" Kace asked, knowing we were all supposed to be done by then.

"I…um…I'm always swamped with paperwork for Gary," I lied again.

Kace gave me a look, like he didn't believe me, but he didn't argue. He usually left right after his innings, so he didn't know what I did and when.

Once we hung up with my brother, Kace gave me one last look, hugged me, and then vowed to go back to ignoring my existence. He left, and I waited about ten more minutes before opening my door again, ensuring Kace was long gone. Slipping out, wearing my nighty shorts, an oversized King's t-shirt, and slippers, I made my way up to Chase's room.

He didn't know I was coming, and I wasn't even sure he was there. He may have even been asleep. But I knew he would be happy to see me.

So when he opened his door and leaned on the frame, I didn't expect his eyes to be so stony.

"Uh, hey."

"Hey," he replied coolly, not moving to let me inside.

"Um, you okay?"

"Yep." His arm held the door open but he still didn't move. The thought, that maybe I should have called him first, ran through my head.

"Can I come in?"

He stared at me for a long minute and I got fidgety, knowing Kace's room was right across the hall. When I started looking around Chase huffed and brought my attention back to him.

"He got back ten minutes ago."

"Who?"

"You know who, *Becs*."

Becs? No one called me Becs except…

My eyes widened, and I looked back at Kace's door. When I looked back at Chase, he was closing his door on me, not giving me a chance to explain.

"Wait!" I yelled and slipped under his arm before he could finish shutting the door.

"What are you doing?"

"Explaining." Although, I wasn't sure how much I had to explain. Or if I even owed him an explanation.

Chase stood there, his arms crossed, waiting for me to talk. But words didn't come. He was in low hanging sweatpants, no shirt, and his hair was a mess. He was distracting, I wasn't going to be able to explain anything until I shook off his effect on my brain.

Walking farther into the room, I stopped and gasped, seeing the broken plate and carrot cake all over the window and floors.

"What happened?" I asked, turning to look back at him.

"Guess I was a little frustrated," he shrugged.

"Why?"

"Well, *Becs*, why don't you tell me how you know Kace Jackson?"

My eyes widened in shock, but I knew when he called me Becs that he must have found out.

"He's a player on your team," I joked, but also gauging how much he knew.

"Stop lying," he warned. "I was headed to your room with that carrot cake when he stopped by himself."

"He's friends with my family. He was just worried about me earlier."

"Why have you never mentioned that?"

"Same reason I didn't tell him that you and I went to Disney World," I spoke louder, upset that he was upset. Partly because he knew, and partly because he shouldn't have cared. "What does it matter to you?"

"Don't play dumb, Princess, you know why!"

"I have told you a million times that this job is hard, especially for a woman. The ball to the head was proof of that. I didn't want to be associated with anyone here. He didn't help me get this job; he didn't even know I applied. I asked him before we came to pretend he didn't know me. If everyone knew that I knew him, they would think I got this job because of him, and not on my own merit. And if I got a long-term job, they would think it was because of him, too. So I had to lie."

Chase took in what I was saying but still seemed annoyed. He shook his head silently several times, looking off at the wall beside him before finally letting go of some of his anger. "I get that. And I have no right to be upset, and I have no right to care. But I can't help it."

"I know," I assured him. We were becoming attached and we shouldn't have been. It was a line we had been walking on for several days, both afraid to cross it entirely.

"How's the bump?" he asked with a grimace, simultaneously ending the argument and switching into a concerned mode. Guilt was all over his face as well. "I should have asked that first, I'm sorry."

"Not bad. No concussion. Just a knot."

He ran a hand down his face, and I noted how weary he looked. The stress was more evident the longer I was there and I decided that I needed to let him be for a while.

"I'll go, Chase. I didn't want to upset you. I just wanted to see you for some reason. And this was my first chance. Sorry I didn't tell you about Kace." Which was another lie. I wasn't sorry. I was just sorry I got caught. I would have told him the whole truth if I was really sorry. I may have cared about Chase on a deeper level than I should, but I wasn't quite ready for that conversation. And not because he would get mad, but because I was too scared it would change things between us. Despite how much we shouldn't have been doing any of the things we were doing, I didn't want it to stop.

"Don't go," he whispered, raising his head to look at me. "Sorry I overreacted about Kace. I think I was...am...was... am...." he sighed, looking like he didn't want to finish the thought but did, "jealous."

His admission caused warmth to spread through me and I smiled. *Jealous?* Jealousy wasn't supposed to be an attractive quality in a man, but there I was, finding everything about Chase Turner appealing.

"Can you help me keep that a secret?" I dared to ask, referring to Kace. "I don't even want him knowing you know. I want nothing more than to go back to pretending I have no idea who Kace Jackson is."

"I will lie through my teeth, Princess." My relief must have been written all over my face because he pulled me into his arms. "Come 'ere." He hugged me and kissed my bump, but with less subtlety than he did in Gary's office. Laying my cheek on his bare chest, I soaked in his warmth.

"I bet that carrot cake was good," I finally said, enjoying the way his chest moved as he laughed at my comment.

"I will order another one," he said but didn't move.

"How's your knee?"

"It's okay, maybe two nights off from PT was just what it needed."

As far as my head was concerned, I was fine, but Gary told me to take all the time off I needed to heal. But my head was fine compared to the hit my pride took.

"I don't know when I'll be back, maybe in a few days," I confessed.

He held on tighter and rubbed up and down my back. "Yeah princess, you take all the time you need. I can handle the workouts alone at this point anyway."

"Speaking of handling things alone. I really do need to go, I'm starving. I almost forgot how to feed myself since you've been providing my meals every night."

"I can order something here, just stay for a bit, please," he begged.

Begging had just been added to my new made-up list of red flags, other unusual things, that I shouldn't have found sexy. Forearms, jealousy, and begging.

"Okay." I smiled, swooning over the sweet way he said 'please.'

He gave me one last squeeze and backed away from our hug before pressing a button on the phone.

"Can I get a hamburger, medium, no cheese, no pickles, no onions, with seasoned fries, and vitamin water?" I was not surprised he knew exactly what I wanted. He had brought us burgers one night to the stadium, and we spent several minutes hashing out the intricacies of the perfect burger. "Can you add a carrot cake to that please?"…"Yes, another one. Thank you."

Looking over at the mess of the original carrot cake, I shook my head, thinking of how sexy it was that he made that mess because of me. Someone was going to have to save me because I was falling for Chase in a way that didn't seem healthy.

When he sat beside me on the bed, he rubbed his thumb gently across the bump on my head again. In his eyes, I saw his guilt over what happened seeping back in, so I grabbed his hand and held it.

"It isn't your fault," I whispered.

He sighed, but I didn't let go of his hand, or let him turn away from me. "I made you a target."

"No, *they* made me a target," I replied. "You know what hurts worse than the knot? The fact that those women couldn't see another woman working in a man's world and root for her. Cheer her on. Why do women not empower one another more? Shouldn't they have been proud that I was out there, kicking ass?"

"You are kicking ass, that's for sure."

"I'm trying. But I'm not being the person I thought I would be when I got here."

"And that is definitely my fault, right?"

I was still holding onto his hand and looked up into his eyes. "Probably."

"I should probably regret that, huh?" He smiled.

"Probably," I repeated, moving in closer, deciding I was going to kiss him.

But I didn't make it very far. A loud knock on the door made me jump back.

"Room Service." That was fast, way too fast.

Chase jumped back, too, standing and heading to the door. He carried my food into the room and placed the tray beside me on the bed.

"Eat up, baby," he whispered. "And don't leave, don't move."

"Where are you going?"

"I need to take a quick shower," he explained.

Nodding, I watched him turn quickly toward the bathroom and shut the door behind him. It was late, and I was starving, but after two bites, exhaustion settled in and I laid back on his pillow and stared at the ceiling. He didn't have to worry about me leaving, or even moving. There wasn't anywhere else I wanted to be.

Even if nothing could come of us, I wanted to stay there, with him, as long as I could.

I woke up saturated in warmth—the smell of soap and spice permeating my sleepy brain. I nuzzled my nose into the wall in front of me, knowing it wasn't exactly a wall. It was Chase's hard chest.

With his arms wrapped around me, and my face pressed

against him, I was more content than I had ever been. While he was showering, I had fallen asleep and woke fleetingly to hear him cleaning the cake from the floor and window. Then he moved my tray of uneaten food to the table and climbed into bed beside me, pulling me into the crook of his body.

At some point, I must have turned to face him and cuddled into his body. All I could think of in that moment, was that heaven must have been something similar.

No light was shining through the window, so I knew it was early, but for Chase and me, it was time to start our day to ensure his knees were good to go.

"Morning." Chase's voice was deep and raspy from sleep.

"Morning. You ready to get to work?"

He buried his head back onto mine and squeezed me tighter, moaning, "Nooooo."

Wishing we didn't have to move, I burrowed my cheek back into his chest and giggled. We laid still for several more minutes, and if it wasn't for hearing his erratic heartbeat, I would have thought he had fallen back to sleep.

My arms were curled between us, and I started brushing my fingers softly along his chest, testing our willpower. His stuttering breath was the only indication he gave me that he was affected, staying still and quiet. I couldn't see his face, but I imagined his eyes were closed, as were mine, soaking everything in.

When I stopped moving my fingers, it was the break he needed to find the power to pull away. He took a deep breath and kissed the top of my head before getting up.

"I gotta stretch," was all he said before disappearing for a minute, never looking back at me.

He was only gone a few minutes before he returned fully clothed and ready. Nothing seemed off, but sleeping in his arms, in his bed, didn't make me feel like *normal* was the way it should have been. I embraced it, though, and got through the stretching routine as best as possible before returning to my room to prepare for the day.

Up until I woke up, I thought I would take Gary up on his offer to take some time off. But I didn't want the other interns to pull ahead in the race for a permanent position. It was important that I got back out there and didn't show weakness.

becca

"Becca, good heavens, what are you doing here?" Gary asked when I popped into his office to let him know I was working.

"This little bump won't keep me away," I smiled.

"Looks pretty rough, you sure you don't need a few days?"

"It looks rough, but I feel fine. I just wanted to let you know I was here before I got to work." I started to turn and leave, eager to get back to normal, but he stopped me.

"Wait. Actually, there's something I need to talk to you about."

Immediately, I assumed he figured out how big of a liar I had become—it was always the first thing I thought of. As the lies accumulated, I became increasingly panicky whenever Gary needed to *talk*.

"Yeah?" I asked, turning back and trying to sound casual.

"It's kind of about Fernandez," he started. Turning ghost-like, an apology sat on the tip of my tongue. The only plan I had was to beg for forgiveness, but he kept talking before I could. "We were very impressed that you caught on to the fluid he carried on that knee. Even more impressed that you didn't let his temper tantrum deter you from doing what was right."

Was he serious?

"We are losing two catchers today. It's just that part of spring training where the guys get cut."

"Okay, so you want me to spend more time with the four that are still here?"

"Well, there's more. Jason, one of the other interns, is also being sent home." *What?* Was that normal? I didn't know we could be cut like the players were. "He was involved in some misconduct. We have rules and regulations. He broke them so he was sent home. We have too many people vying for positions to tolerate disrespect for the rules."

"Right, of course," I nodded, still in disbelief and a whole lot of guilt. I wondered if Jason had broken as many rules as I had. I wondered how long it would be until I got caught, too.

"So, we were prepared for you to take a few days off, but if you think you're ready, we need to add a few players to your workload."

"Yes, that's no problem, Gary." And it wasn't, it was a relief. "Let me know what you need, and I'll get started."

"Well, since you're losing two catchers, I'm going to give you two pitchers. And because we have been so impressed with your work, I'm giving you our number one and number two pitchers."

Oh wow. That was a big deal. Pitchers were the cream of the crop when it came to their physical wellbeing. They battled just as many injuries as anyone else, but their minor injuries could affect so much when it came to their performance.

"Ethan Jones and Eddie Banks? I can handle that, no problem. I will go talk to them this morning."

"One more thing. Since you're going to be here, Jones pitches today and has been battling that blister between his fingers. I want you on the bench today for the game to keep an eye on it."

Damnit.

Thanking Gary for the vote of confidence, I promised to see him in the dugout later, then finally escape his office. Even though I didn't normally head straight to the locker room in the mornings, I wanted to find Ethan and Eddie.

Before opening the door, I sent a little prayer up that the guys had their junk covered and then took the chance. The first thing I noticed were the empty lockers from the guys that had been sent home. It wasn't just the two catchers, but infielders, outfielders, and a few pitchers.

The second thing I noticed was Chase talking to Kace in the corner of the room. Their heads were down and they were laughing. I just hoped they were keeping their promises to me and not letting the other know my secrets.

The lies were mounting. They were everywhere. They were getting complicated. And when

they both looked up at me simultaneously, I froze. *Shit.* They quickly walked away from one another, laughing at what I assumed was me, and I wanted to scream.

Stomping past Chase without even looking at him, I hoped to show how mad I was. It spoke volumes that I didn't look because his shirt was off and his baseball pants were hanging low on his waist without a belt on yet. He was so hot.

Okay, I looked.

But he didn't see me.

When I got past him, I saw Ethan and Eddie, their lockers right by one another. With them together, my mission was easier and I could get the hell out of there quicker.

"Hey, guys. Can I talk to you for a minute?"

They both looked my way and smiled, making me feel at ease. Ethan and I had already spoken, but I was unsure about Eddie. Luckily, he seemed just as nice as Ethan, even asking me about my head before I could tell them what I needed.

"Head is good. I'm fine. Look, I wanted to let you two know that I'm taking over your training care. Jason was let go last night."

Their gasps at the Jason news told me they were as shocked as I was. It was hard to wrap our heads around.

"Okay, sounds good," Eddie nodded. "We will let you know when we need anything."

"Yes, do that. Oh, and Ethan? I'll be on the bench to keep an eye on that blister today. Can you come to see me before you head out to warm up?"

"Yes ma'am," he nodded.

They seemed more manageable than I feared. Pitchers were sometimes the wariest of small changes, but both Ethan and Eddie were good-natured and okay with the change.

As I turned to leave the locker room, I felt relief spread through me, but I was still anxious to get out of there. Without looking, I hurried through the locker room, but ran right into a hard and strong body, which made me whip my head up.

Cam. He was standing there in jeans and a t-shirt, hands coming out to steady me. "Oh, sorry ma'am, I didn't see you."

I scowled at him without saying a word. If my calculations were correct, he had to have flown to Florida overnight, because when I was on Facetime with him and Ali the night before, he was in his damn house. He told me he wouldn't be coming for another week.

The frustration I felt at Chase, and maybe Kace, that morning was amplifying. Why was Cam there? Why was he making me crazy?

Not bothering with a response, I marched off and continued toward the training room. I plowed through the door and slammed my hand on one of the plastic-covered tables, catching the attention of the guys around me—the remaining interns. At least I knew none of them were named Jason.

"You okay?"

"Yep," I answered shortly.

"Guess you heard about Jason?"

"Yep," I answered again, sounding like a bitch. *Dang, Becca, get it together.* "Sorry," I muttered. "It's been a weird morning."

"Yeah, it's been a weird couple of days for you."

Putting my hand up to feel the knot, I nodded my agreement. Thankfully, my head covered up for my mood, and I was able to get on with my morning with everyone just thinking I was mad about the knot.

After I managed to get two of the catcher's ankles wrapped and helped the guys with some paperwork, I had another shit-show to deal with.

"Yo, Princess." Chase was calling me from across the room. Not that I looked, but who else would call me Princess? Who else had such a sexy voice that my knees weakened when I heard it?

It was asinine and completely unfounded, but I was still mad about him *maybe* talking to Kace about knowing me.

"Cupcake!" he called again when I didn't answer.

"What?" I asked without looking up.

"I was just in Gary's office, and he told me to send you in there if I saw you."

Did he see me? Or did he find me? Did it matter? I was over-analyzing everything that morning and needed to get a grip.

"Thanks."

He nodded and walked out while I gathered the papers I was taking notes on. As I left, I passed the other interns, who were looking at me wondering why Gary needed me.

Hell, if I knew.

When I got to Gary's office, the first thing I noticed was that Gary wasn't there. "What the—" I started but was pushed from behind into the office, Chase closing the door behind us.

"What's wrong, Princess?" he asked, folding his arms over his chest.

"Does Gary need me? I need to go find him."

"No, he's on the field. I just needed to talk to you. What's wrong?"

"What do you mean? I'm working."

"Noooo, your face was fine, and then it wasn't, and your eyes are darker. The whole time you were in the locker room, you were short and cold. That isn't like you." *He noticed all that?*

"I saw you talking to Kace. You two were all buddy-buddy and laughing. Then you both saw me and separated. Laughing." I turned to walk back and forth, something to do in case I sounded like a sulky child. Cause I knew there was a chance I was over-reacting.

"Are we not allowed to talk?" Chase asked.

"Did you tell him you knew?"

"What? *No*. We weren't even talking about you," he practically yelled.

"Then why did you both laugh after looking at me?"

"Geez Baby, he was just telling me a friend of ours was in town. That he was gonna stop by the locker room this morning to say hey, but wanted to know if I wanted to have drinks with them later."

"So you didn't tell him you knew?"

"No, I promised you I wouldn't, and I didn't," his tone softened. "I don't want you being kicked out of here. Everything between you and me is a secret."

"Kace looked at me too, at the exact same time."

"I can't answer for him, but he didn't say anything to me about you either. He kept your secret safe."

In my gut, I knew I had been overreacting so I sighed in frustration and embarrassment. Being upset with him was safer. It was like building a wall of protection for myself. But it was crumbling as quickly as I built it.

"Who's the friend?" I asked in curiosity, but somehow already knowing the answer.

"Cam Nichols. You know him too?" he teased.

"Nope," I lied and turned away to hide my eyes.

"Hey, come here."

I wasn't ready to look up, but I turned back around and headed closer to him. When I was sure my eyes had forgotten their lying ways, I looked up.

Chase was devastatingly gorgeous. His intense stare took my breath away whenever I got that close to him. "Better?"

"Yeah, sorry. I just... This," I pointed to my head. "And that," I gestured to the door, not indicating anything in particular. "It's been a weird morning." That line worked with the other guys, so I stuck with it.

Chase pulled me into a hug and rested his chin on the top of my head. Wrapping my arms around his waist, I took a deep breath. Unlike earlier in the locker room, he had his jersey on, and the buttons dug into my cheek.

My phone started buzzing in my pocket and even though I didn't want to acknowledge it, Chase felt it and pulled away.

"I'll let you get that, Princess. I gotta go to work, Ethan is waiting for me in the 'pen."

Nodding quietly, I backed away as the buzzing from my phone stopped.

"Hey," Chase said, gently touching my face. His thumb skimmed my cheek and I locked my eyes onto his. He never finished whatever he was going to say, just kissed my head again and left.

The heat his kiss created made the pain from the knot barely noticeable. It almost made me forget that I had missed a call, but then my phone started buzzing again.

Ali.

"You are one big ass liar," I growled, instead of a cordial "hello."

"How do you know?" she screeched tand laughed.

"I ran into, literally ran into, your boyfriend, in the locker room this morning."

"Which one?" Ali asked.

"Which one would I be shocked to see right now?"

"Okay, so I can explain," she giggled. "After we got off the phone with you, Kace called us again when he got back to his room. I was missing him so much. Cam suggested we just hop on a charter flight and head down. So, we really came to see Kace, not you."

"Whatever," I muttered, knowing that was most likely the truth.

"But I'm calling because, well, Cam went with Kace to the stadium, as you know, and they're also planning a few beers at the bar tonight. I'm sleeping all day and then thought you and I should take the chance to have that dinner downtown we talked about. Just us girls."

Dinner with my best friend sounded perfect. I needed some time away from the hotel and the team. Disney didn't count because Chase was there, and truthfully, I needed time away from him, too. My feelings for him were getting stronger, and hoped some time apart would abate them a little, and make them more manageable.

"Yes!" I squealed. "I need until 7:30 or so, a late dinner, okay?"

"Of course! I have a car service so I will meet you out front. Sound good?"

"As long as no one sees you and me getting to the car," I dead-panned. "I don't need questions being asked."

"I will be waiting in the car, promise."

Now, all I had to do was make sure Chase didn't bring dinner to our session tonight, and find some time to grab a change of clothes from the hotel.

First, I had to survive a day in the dugout and keep an eye on Ethan.

chase

BECCA WAS SITTING THREE FEET TO MY RIGHT. HOW THE FUCK WAS I supposed to get up and walk on that field when she was within reach?

Gary put her on the bench to keep an eye on Ethan. I'd have explained to him that I slept with her in my arms and couldn't shake the feeling of how good it felt, but that didn't seem like a good idea. He probably wouldn't have understood my need to separate her and the game. It was important that I focused solely on catching Ethan, and all I could think about was her shampoo and soft skin.

And her fingers making those small strokes on my chest before we got up. There should have been an award ceremony for me for having the strength to pull away and get up. It took every-thing I had to not run my hand down the curve of her hips, down her legs, back up again, and cup her under her—

"Earth to Turner."

Fuck. I was broken.

"What?" I snapped, trying to find who was calling my name.

"You wanna head to the bullpen? I need to warm up, the game is in thirty minutes." *Ethan.* He was talking to me like I was an idiot–slowly–as if I couldn't understand the words coming from his mouth. With my knee pads and chest protector on, sitting in the dugout, didn't he know I was definitely ready?

Without answering him, though, I looked at Becca, who started paying attention to Ethan. She was holding his hand, touching his fingers one at a time, and running soft circles over one of his blisters.

"Yep, let's go." I stood so quickly that I almost knocked Ethan over while also grabbing his non-pitching arm and dragging him away. I was ready to get to work. Or perhaps I didn't want Becca touching Ethan. We may never know.

Once I was out of the dugout and away from Becca's orbit, the warm-up went smoothly and I settled into what I had to do. Then we returned to the dugout, stood for the national anthem, and took the field, all while keeping my head in the game.

By the fourth inning, Ethan's pitches started finding more dirt and air than the actual strike zone, and I knew his fingers were burning up again. As did Coach. And probably Gary. So I wasn't surprised at all to see Coach call time out and come check on him. But I was more than shocked to see Becca following him.

Becca may have been on the bench that day, but Gary had some nerve sending her onto the same field she was attacked on just the day before. As I walked to the mound to meet them, I felt protective and wanted to walk her back to the safety of the dugout. Maybe even tell Gary where he could shove his—

Who the fuck was I right now?

"Jones," Coach grumbled. "What's going on?"

"Let me see the blister," Becca said, softer than Coach, as she reached for his hand. She turned it over and looked a few times before she spoke again. "You need to come in and let me patch this up before it opens and gets gross."

She was so sweet and nurturing toward Ethan, yet, she threatened to take my balls off when it was *me* she was talking to. Of course, she had already removed my balls and stored them neatly in her pocket, which was precisely why I started nodding in agreement with her. Even though I knew Ethan wanted to finish the inning, and it wasn't actually my call, I was all, "*Yep, Princess is right.*" Ethan was set to argue, too, but once I loaned my support to *Team Becca*, he relented and followed her into the dugout.

I followed her as well…with my eyes. Watching as she and my balls made their way into the tunnel toward the locker room.

After three more innings, I came out of the game and Fernandez finished up. Without stretching my knees or doing a cooldown on the field, I went straight to the locker room and grabbed my phone. A missed call from my housekeeper, Isla, and two texts from Becca stared back at me. Even though Isla was probably calling me about my dad, I still checked my texts first.

> Don't worry about dinner tonight. I'm meeting a friend after we have our sesh.
>
> I quickly ran back to the hotel for a change of clothes. If you get this before I return, it would be safe to assume you didn't stretch… stretch your damn knees.

How did she know I would skip my stretches? Sending her a quick laughing emoji and then a thumbs up, I clicked out of her message and prepared myself for my call to Isla.

"Hey, what's up?" I asked when Isla answered the phone. I had taken a few minutes to get out of my uniform and out of the locker room so no one heard me.

"Mr. Turner, thank goodness. I came in today and your father is gone, missing." She was practically screaming.

"Wait, what?" I shouted a little too loud, in disbelief.

"He's gone!" she repeated.

"Are my cars gone?" There was no worry about the cars themselves, but if he decided to drive again, I would never forgive him if he hurt someone.

"No, I hid the keys, as you said. I saw all the cars, but he is not here."

"Okay, okay…" I softened my voice, trying to assure her it was okay. Isla was a sixty-year-old woman with grown kids and a sick husband. She didn't need me asking her to worry about my dad any more than she already was. She had been asked to feed him, help him, and see that he had the things he needed. That was more than enough. If he left my apartment, that wasn't her responsibility.

"Mr. Turner, I should do something!"

"No." Taking a deep breath, I tried to stay calm. Looking toward the ground, I ran a hand through my hair and then pinched the bridge of my nose. "Isla, there's nothing to worry about. Okay? I promise. I will see you when I get home."

It was all I could say and do. Leaving Florida wasn't an option, and technically, my father was a grown man. He was allowed to go where he wanted. I couldn't save him.

After I hung up with Isla I was past caring about my knees. All I wanted to do was lie down until I was supposed to meet up with Becca. With the way my head was feeling though, meeting up with her wasn't a good idea. She didn't need to know about my dad and I would be too tempted to tell her and wallow in self-pity.

Canceling tonight. I will stretch on my own.

Waiting a minute, I expected her to text me back but nothing ever came through. Not even those little bubbles showing me she was typing something. By the time I got to the hotel, there was still no word from her. Even after I laid down for a bit, she had yet to text me back. I wasn't exactly worried, but something definitely felt off.

Then I got up and went for a drive, hoping I cleared my head once and for all. After three hours of roaming, I ended up with four pamphlets for rehabs, two Snickers bars, and a hard lemonade that I downed in one gulp once I was back in the parking garage.

None of those seemed to fix my craziness.

So, I gave up and went back to my room until it was time to meet the guys for drinks.

I walked into the lobby around 7:30 that night and immediately saw Kace and Cam taking turns kissing their girl, Ali. It looked like they were saying their goodbyes, and when I walked up, I heard Ali saying, "I'm off to be the Isla slayer, wish me luck."

"Isla?" I asked. That wasn't a common name, and the odds of hearing it twice in one day were slim.

Ali jumped, not realizing I was behind her.

"Oh, Chase, hey. Good to see you."

"You too. What's an Isla slayer?" I asked, curious but trying not to be rude.

Ali just waved a hand at me and rolled her eyes. "No biggie. A friend of mine just seems to have a new and sudden aversion to the name. I haven't gotten the details yet, but I can tell I will need to slay some dragons tonight. Have fun guys."

She walked out of the hotel as I shrugged, letting it go, and turned to the guys. "Ready?"

"Yep," they nodded. "You're driving since you somehow got your car here."

"Fuckers." I laughed and led the way out to my car.

becca

"So let me get this straight. You overheard him on the phone, talking to an 'Isla', and he said he would see her when he got home?"

Ali wasn't just my best friend, she was my therapist. But I was trying to be as vague as possible and that wasn't my best idea. It led to a whole lot of confusion and assumptions. She was already suspicious that I was crushing on a player, and I had to lie through my teeth to try and convince her he was a random guy I met who was in town for a few days. There was just no way I could risk telling her about Chase. I'd have to ask her to keep it from Kace and that wasn't fair.

Being vague was my only way of getting her thoughts after accidentally overhearing Chase on the phone. When I returned to the stadium, after getting my clothes, he was backed down a corridor trying to be discreet as he talked on the phone. I didn't hear much, but the name Isla suddenly made me want to throw up.

'Isla, there's nothing to worry about. Okay? I promise. I will see you when I get home.'

Home.

Chase wasn't married, but that didn't mean he didn't have a girlfriend waiting for him back home. Probably a jealous girlfriend that he had to reassure and comfort.

Why did I care? I didn't have a claim on him. We were nothing to each other.

Lies.

We were something. Something we hadn't acted on or labeled, but we both knew it was there. Maybe *she* was why he pulled away. Maybe that was why he seemed to be stronger than I was.

"Yep," I finally said to Ali and sipped my martini.

"That doesn't mean anything, she could be his mom."

"A mom he calls Isla?" I shook my head. "Plus his mom is dead."

"You two know each other well enough to know about families and such?"

I stayed quiet and shrugged, not wanting to risk her realizing I was talking about Chase.

"What's the deal here? You really like this guy, huh?"

"I don't know, it's complicated. There's something that sizzles around us, but it's kind of a bad idea. I think I keep trying to find reasons to be mad at him, or hate him."

Ali eyed me over the rim of her glass. She knew. I could see it in her eyes. She knew I was lusting after a player, and that was why it was a terrible idea. But she didn't press for more. She let me be.

She would probably tell Kace and Cam, but she didn't have a name or anything, so she may let me off the hook for a while. There had to be some sort of best friend code she wouldn't break, right?

Thankfully, the rest of the night wasn't about me and my irrational worries. We managed to keep other subjects and conversations going the rest of the time. When the night ended, Ali's driver dropped me off at the side of the hotel like I had asked, so no one saw us together.

The plan was to go straight to my room and go to bed. But I was tempted to go to Chase's room. Ali had gotten a text from Cam that the guys had already called it a night and were back at the hotel, so I knew Chase was there. Somehow, I resisted and ordered an Uber instead.

Twenty minutes later, I was at the stadium, flashing my employee badge to the nighttime security guard and entering the dark, quiet locker room. There was no reason I should have been there, but the thought crossed my mind that I could catch up on paperwork. Paperwork seemed endless. The other thought I had was to change into some clothes I left in my locker and exercise a bit.

I did none of that.

Instead, I sat on Chase's stool next to his locker and willed the locker to tell me all his secrets. All I did was stare, being sure not to touch anything, just taking stock of the contents I could see.

He had four clean jerseys hanging up. Athletic shorts and t-shirts folded at the top. Each locker had a safe for personal items, but his was wide open. *Nothing to hide away while he wasn't here.* At the bottom, he had two pairs of cleats, tennis shoes, and flip-flops. On a small shelf were his deodorant, body wash, and a small picture of an older woman with his same dark eyes. His mom, I assumed.

None of it said, "*Hey, I have a girlfriend at home,*" but I tried to dissect it all anyway.

"Creeping around?" His deep voice sounded behind me, startling me. I didn't have to look to know it was Chase, so I kept my head turned toward his locker and shrugged. It wasn't like I could talk properly when I was kind of irrationally mad at him for having a girlfriend named Isla back at home waiting on him —maybe.

Yeah, I wasn't sure of that, but I *needed* to hate him.

"You at my locker for a reason?" Another question I didn't want to answer but that time, I did.

"No," I lied.

He started walking closer, and his voice turned from teasing to tender. "You upset about something, Baby? I swear I stretched my knee when I got to my room."

Baby.

"Why are you here?" What were the odds he and I both ended up in that same spot at the same time?

"I asked you first."

His hands were in his pockets and he looked so good in his jeans and button-up top—the sleeves rolled to his elbows. His hair was perfectly coiffed, and his eyes were deep with concern.

When he got close enough, he squatted down to my level, much like he did every day as a catcher. His hand rested on my knee to keep himself steady, and he squeezed.

"What's wrong?" he whispered, asking again.

I was being ridiculous. I didn't know who Isla was. I had just decided she was his girlfriend, which upset me. And as guilty as I would feel about sleeping in the arms of another woman's man, I realized I was more upset that if he had a girlfriend, then that meant he was unavailable. He would never be more to me than he was in that moment.

That should have been a blessing. Taking the choice away from me would make it easier to escape because I was slowly breaking down every time I was with him. It was only a matter of time before my world blew up because of him.

"I went to get my clothes so I could change after work. When I got back to the stadium, I walked up and heard you on the phone around the corner, assuring Isla that you would see her when you got home. I didn't stick around and that's all I heard. But it pretty much made me think you have someone back in Atlanta."

As much as it sucked, I told him the truth for once. Not just about my assumptions, making it pretty clear where my feelings were as well.

Jealousy.

Madness.

Sulkiness.

I thought he would look disconcerted, maybe a little chagrined at being caught.

But he was smiling. Fucking. Smiling.

Pushing his hand off my knee, I stood and walked to the door that led to the dugout. It was a chilly night, and I was in my sundress, but I needed air.

As I expected, Chase was right on my tail, following my every step without a word. When we got to the empty dugout, Chase spun me to look at him, still smiling bigger than I thought was possible.

"Are you jealous?"

His pompous attitude enraged me and I couldn't keep quiet. "Why would I be jealous when there isn't anything to be jealous of? We aren't a thing, Chase. We are nothing. But I'm a little disappointed in you. I'm disappointed that you ended up being the kind of man who takes other women to Disney World and sleeps with them in your bed when you have someone at home waiting for you to return!"

My speech made him full-on belly laugh and he was holding his side while shaking his head. Stomping off again, I headed onto the field, not even sure if I was allowed to be out there at this time of night. My heels started falling deep into the grass, making it hard to walk, so I took them off and walked barefoot toward the outfield.

When I got as far as right field, Chase caught up to me. "Becca, wait!" He still had amusement in his voice, but his use of my actual name caused me to halt.

"This isn't funny, Chase. I'm so embarrassed. I'm just thankful that I realized this before I ruined my career and did something stupid."

He sobered up, suddenly getting serious. "First of all, Isla is my housekeeper. Not my girlfriend. And I will see her when I get home—every day from six am to two pm. Because she cleans my house and shit." I started to speak, but he kept going, cutting me off. "Second of all, you're wrong. There is something between us. We *are* a thing. I'm not completely sure what that *thing* is yet, but it's been inevitable since I laid eyes on you."

He took a deep breath, and I remained silent, debating whether I believed him. I had no reason not to believe him. I knew before I even started going crazy on him that I was jumping to conclusions. But those conclusions were supposed to save me. I needed them to be true.

"Lastly, Baby. Just stop. Stop thinking about stupid decisions. We have already made them. We are already in too deep, and you know it."

"We haven't crossed the line of no return," I mumbled.

"I have," he tapped his chest. "I've been done for since your face lit up at the sight of Disney World. Or probably when you threatened my balls in the dugout. Shit, maybe it was when I held your hand, right over there," he pointed to where we had laid the other night, looking at the stars, "and you thanked me for not kissing you."

Chase ran a hand through his hair as he looked at the sky and then continued. "For fuck's sake, Becca, it may not feel like it, but I have been doing everything I can to make sure you know how I feel about you without risking your career any more than I already am. I wish I could save you. But I can't. And I'm done trying."

"Done?" I croaked, my heart was beating rapidly as I trembled from every word he spoke. My heart knew everything he was saying was true. It was the truth that we had been lying to ourselves about for weeks.

"It's up to you now. You tell me to walk away and I will. You tell me not to kiss you and I won't. But I'm done making the decisions. You're gonna have to save yourself now."

Kiss me? He was going to kiss me, I could see it in his eyes, and it was my turn to be strong. Walking away was easy to do when I was mad or upset, but doing it while knowing he was going to kiss me? I didn't have the strength.

"When I shook your hand," I spoke in almost a whisper, making Chase look a little confused. "That's when I crossed the line of no return. When I shook your hand in the locker room that first day." Since we had never been intimate, I thought the lines that we *had* crossed were safe. But Chase was right and the point of no return was long gone. No matter how much we denied the physical aspect of our relationship, it didn't change the chemistry between us. It didn't change the way we felt. So I answered him with the truth: I was unequivocally lost to him the moment I touched him.

Two steps closer and Chase was directly in front of me, holding my neck and tilting my face to his. "Stop me, baby."

Adamantly, I shook my head with surrender in my eyes. "I can't."

Without any hesitation, his lips were on mine and his tongue found the seam, begging for entrance into my mouth. I opened willingly. Helplessly. He held my face to his and devoured my lips like he had been starving. My hands wrapped around his forearms, trying to get closer to him despite there being no more space between us. I hadn't realized how close we had gotten to the outfield wall until he backed me up against the wall's padding and pressed his body into mine, holding me up with his strength.

He took his right hand from my neck and grabbed my thigh, pulling it up around his waist so he could rock into me and show me how hard his cock was. We had joked about his "boners," but that was not one of those times. It was primal and instinctual. He needed me to know what I did to him.

Unconsciously, I ground my pussy on him, seeking friction between our clothing. When he realized what I needed, he grabbed my other thigh and wrapped both legs around his waist, opening me further so I could feel him against me. The relief I felt at finally being *there* with him was overwhelming and I had to peel my lips from his just to breathe.

"Please," I whispered into his ear, as his lips moved to my neck. He groaned with my plea and brought his forehead to mine, his breathing erratic.

"Now, please," I begged against his lips. "I need you."

That was all he needed to hear to take one of his hands between us and loosen his belt. With just one hand, he was going too slow for me, so I reached and pulled his zipper down on his jeans. They loosened just enough to allow him to free his cock and I wrapped my hand around his thickness and squeezed.

Chase's responding growl was almost wild, making his chest vibrate as I stroked him. Then he reached under my dress and slid my panties to the side, touching me and sliding one finger inside me to feel how wet I was.

"Are you always this wet for me, Cupcake? Do you walk around in those work khakis, praying this wet pussy doesn't leave a mark for everyone to see?"

"Oh God," I moaned as he teased me.

"Think of all those times my cock has been begging for you. Wishing you would touch me above the fucking knee. Stroke me. Now your tiny hand is trying to hold on tight and I'm fucking losing my mind."

"Chase?" I cried. "Don't make us wait anymore."

Pulling his finger from my pussy, he swatted my hand off his dick and lined himself up to my core. Instead of looking at me, he was looking at our connection, and I started to tremble as he bit his lip in anticipation. When he pushed inside of me, he started slow, but then finished by practically impaling me and I screamed with relief.

"You okay?"

"Oh God, yes."

He brought our faces together, our lips only a breath apart, as he slowly moved in and out of my channel. Every few strokes, he would push hard and I seethed from the sensation.

"I don't want to hurt you," he whispered. "But I'm losing my fucking control."

"You won't hurt me."

"Promise me you'll stop me if I do?"

Without waiting for my answer, he moved faster, touching me somewhere so deep that tears started forming in my eyes. Chase was fucking me with a passion and roughness I hadn't been expecting. A desperation that was finally being met with our connection. It was unlike anything I had experienced before.

When he pressed his lips back to mine, I could no longer focus on what my body was doing and I came without any warning. It felt like I was close to blacking out from pleasure as waves of my orgasm took over my entire body.

Clenching on to Chase's cock inside of me, he couldn't hold off either, and started stuttering his pace as I felt him growing inside me. His jerky motions instantly reignited my desire and as my orgasm faded, another sparked and I knew I was going to come again.

"I have to pull out, Princess."

"No," I cried. "Come inside me, Chase."

"Fuck," he growled, then did as I asked, letting go as we came together. Our moans echoed in the empty stadium, drifting off into the open air, making sure anyone that was in the area knew exactly what we were doing against that right field wall.

As the intense feelings started to ebb, we stayed connected with our foreheads together and our arms wrapped around each other. We stayed in that exact position as our breathing started leveling off.

It took a few minutes, but eventually, the blood went back to our brains and Chase slid out of me. My panties snapped back into place as he did, catching his cum as it ran out of my core. With a lazy and satisfied smile, he tucked himself back into his jeans and looked at me as I leaned against the wall with my arms behind me, keeping me steady.

"I'm on the pill," I blurted, which was not very romantic, but very necessary to put out there.

"I trust you." His words made me flinch ever so slightly, but not enough that he noticed.

I had just lied to him—again. I wasn't on the pill. And I had never had sex without a condom. But Chase did that to me. He made me lose all reason and responsibility.

He leaned into me again and kissed me, letting me know that his need for me didn't stop once we came. There was no turning away anymore, no more denying the feelings that had consumed us from day one.

"Let's get out of this stadium."

Agreeing with him, I nodded and took his hand, letting him guide me back through the dugout and to the locker room. He grabbed a few things from his locker and ordered a ride back to the hotel. But once we were there, we went our separate ways. Not for the night, but just long enough to make sure no one saw us.

When I got to my room, I started to change my clothes and wrapped a towel around my body. Chase's soft knock came before I could get completely dressed, though, so I opened the door with just the towel. The same way he had done the first night I showed up at his door.

Chase barely let me close the door before his lips were on mine. He was pulling at the towel, making me drop it and then slightly backed up. Looking at me for the first time, completely bare, his eyes got darker with each pass over my body. Desire was all over his face and I felt like a queen.

"Fuck, you're beautiful," he mumbled, before coming back to my lips. While he worked on getting his belt off again, I tore at his shirt, working the buttons as fast as possible. Our lips were connected, hindering our sight, but our hands knew exactly where to go.

When his shirt was finally open, I pushed it off his shoulders and stood back to look at him the way he had done to me. Even though I had seen him shirtless plenty of times, that time was different. That time was for me.

While I admired his chest, he slipped his jeans off and toed his way out of his socks and shoes. He was completely naked for me, standing there like a statue, like a gift. It was almost hard to believe I had just had him inside me, possessing me. My hands had been on him, my mouth on him, my body pressed against his.

And I wanted more.

Each feeling the same way, we took two steps toward one another and reconnected our lips and bodies. Chase scooped me into his arms and laid me on the bed, hovering over me. His cock was hard, pressing against my sore pussy, letting me know he was ready for more.

"I can take it," I teased him against his lips.

"I want to go slower this time. Savor every inch of you."

His mouth moved to my neck, then my chest, trails of his kisses leading to my nipples. He took one between his teeth and tugged, before flicking it with his tongue as if it was my clit. Below him, I started squirming, anxious for him to be back inside of me. We had spent way too long avoiding what we always should have known would happen, and I wanted to make up for lost time.

"You still have my cum sitting inside your pussy? Waiting for me to fill you back up again?"

"You know I do," I smiled, pressing my chest up to his mouth again.

Taking one finger, he ran it through my folds and then brought it to my lips, pushing it against my tongue and making me suck. I moaned as I tasted our combined flavors and then bit down, making him hiss. He pulled his finger from my mouth and held my jaw still, making sure our eyes were connected as he pushed into me.

"Fuck you're so tight. It's like you were made just for me."

Without closing our eyes, we watched each other as he moved, bringing us closer and closer to another climax. It was intense, and way more intimate than I imagined the night being. But the way his eyes widened and his mouth dropped open a little when he was getting close was better than foreplay. My pussy instantly reacted and I took my nails down his back as I came.

Instead of pushing for me to come again, he followed behind me, filling me back up just like he promised, and making me feel full of not only the evidence of his pleasure, but something else. Something deeper and more profound.

Something I didn't want to even think about because it scared the shit out of me.

CHAPTER NINETEEN

chase

IT WAS LIKE ONCE WE OPENED THE DOOR, THERE WAS NO STOPPING us. Becca and I were both ravenous for each other. Completely unable to slow down and savor the moment.

When I went to the stadium looking for her, I didn't anticipate the outcome being us together against the right field wall. All I knew was that I just wanted to be around her.

I *needed* her.

After a night out with my friends, my dad finally called me. The call was from the Atlanta Police Department, and a little blurry, because I spent most of the time on the phone outside of the bar I was at, yelling, "What the fuck, Dad?"

But I posted the fifty-thousand-dollar bail for his drunken bullshit, had Isla get him, and tried to enjoy the rest of the night with my friends. When I walked back into the bar, I snuck over to the bartender and ordered ten sweet teas. He thought I was crazy but there was no way I could enjoy a buzz from alcohol after that call.

Of course, I didn't want the guys catching on, so they thought it was whiskey. At the rate I was downing that tea, I'm surprised they didn't wonder why I wasn't passed out on the floor. After my ten sweet teas, though, I couldn't take it anymore, so I made a lame excuse about turf toe and left before they could question me. They could find their own way back because I couldn't be around people in the mood I was in.

Becca didn't count as "people." She was the one person I did want to be around.

I needed her.

There was no telling why she had avoided texting me all day, but I was determined to see if she wanted to sleep in my arms again. Just sleep, so I could be near her. Without her knowing how my night had gone, I knew her presence would comfort me.

It took several knocks on her door to realize she wasn't in her room, and something in my gut told me to head to the stadium. I wasn't sure why that was my first instinct, but I wasn't shocked to find her there. What I didn't expect was to see her sitting on my stool in front of my locker, looking at the contents with a snarl. And I was especially thrown off by her sour disposition.

With her being upset, I forgot about my dad quicker than I had imagined possible. I had a whole new problem. It was vital I figured out what had her so upset and fix it immediately.

Her attempt to escape to the field was fruitless because I followed behind her, determined to do whatever she needed from me. But when she finally snapped and ranted about Isla, I couldn't keep the smile off my face.

It's not that I was happy that she was upset. Nor was I upset with her assumptions that she had jumped to without even asking me first. But I was damn elated that she cared. The idea of me having a girlfriend sent her into a frenzy.

Jealousy.

It probably wasn't healthy, but I was happy to see her jealous and frazzled over the idea of me seeing someone. Because it was exactly how I felt when I saw Kace walk into her room. Or when she touched Ethan. It made me feel like we were finally on the same playing field.

Neither one of us could go on like that. It didn't matter if we never touched one another, the damage had been done. We were officially fucked. So, I didn't see any need to back away and pretend we were friends.

We never were.

And when she didn't stop me from kissing her, I was done for. Something had come over me, and I snapped. I didn't exactly anticipate fucking her against the right field wall in the middle of a dark stadium, but consequences be damned, I got inside her, and came inside her.

Trusting her.

Now I had fucked her a few more times and she was laying content on my chest, naked and asleep. My fingers stroked her hair gently as I savored the quiet. It was early morning, and I knew we had to get up for my workout, but the sun wasn't up, and a Florida rainstorm was blowing through. Lightning flashed in the window every so often and those pockets of light allowed me to gaze down at the woman in my arms.

When I first saw her, I knew she belonged in my arms. But I had no idea how incredible it would be, or how addicted I would get. She was beautiful, but also smart and spunky. Ambitious and determined. I wanted to see her succeed in our world of grunts and jocks. I wanted to watch her flourish while putting guys like me, who gave her shit, in their place. I wanted to be the guy who stood beside her and punched the Fernandez's of the world, reminding them how special she was and how dumb it was to speak down to her while I was around.

My jealousy would never work though. I'd have to get over the feelings I had when I saw her touching other guys—like Ethan. Even if it was in the most platonic way. There were too many variables that made relationships in the workplace a bad idea, and jealousy was at the top of the list. Maybe it was possible to get past it as long as I knew I was the one in her bed at night.

My thoughts kept straying from one random thing to the

next until I felt her move under me, bringing me back to her presence in my arms. She gently rubbed her nose on my chest like a soft kiss. My fingers continued in her hair, rubbing methodically—just enough so she knew I was awake.

"How do you smell so good?" she smiled, making my chest rumble with quiet laughter.

"Are you admitting that you lied to me?"

She looked up quickly and widened her eyes. "Lied?"

"Yeah, when you told me I stunk," I reminded her.

She smiled again and laid her head back down on my chest. "Maybe."

But I already knew that.

"It's okay. I've lied to you a few times, too."

"Well, aren't we quite the pair. What do you need to fess up to? Is that perfect hair a toupee? Do you steal signs?"

"None of that." I ticketed her and made her squirm.

"So tell me something true, Chase." She looked up and rested her chin on her hand, looking intently at me.

Since we had started having dinner every night, we had asked each other random questions, like, "What is the perfect vacation?" or "What's the worst pain you've ever felt?" We knew a lot about one another but it felt like she was asking for something deeper, more profound.

"It's not just the money," I confessed out of the blue.

"What else is there?" she playfully asked, knowing exactly what I had meant when I said it.

"I'm old," I started, showing her a slight weakness in my armor. "In baseball years, I have only a few left to play. Especially as a catcher. It won't be long before I'm moved to the bench to back up some younger version with fresh knees, and the kind of stamina I lack."

Becca was quiet as her eyes bounced back and forth between mine. She was so serious that I was afraid I had opened a window

I didn't want to open. I wanted to tell her the truth, but I didn't want her pity or consolation.

"Chase?" she started, sounding unsure. "I probably won't be able to walk today because of your stamina, how in the hell is it lacking?"

"I said in baseball years," I laughed, loving her wit.

"Yeah, whatever. Same thing," she waved.

No, it wasn't the same thing. But she didn't patronize me with "You will be okay" or "Aw, poor Chase." She sat up and straddled me, my hands finding her hips and holding tightly.

Somehow, we had managed to get semi-dressed for bed before falling asleep together, so my boxers and her panties separated us. She had on an oversized King's t-shirt that she liked wearing to bed and it swallowed her whole. Her hair was brought up into a sexy mess on her head and her eyes were fucking criminal with desire.

My cock grew hard as she bit her lip and gently rubbed her pussy over me. "How am I going to go to work today knowing that every time I see you, I will wish we were here, doing this?"

Using my hands, I kept her position on me and pushed her back and forth. "I will call you Princess, and you will sneer at me, and I will piss you off, and you will want to remove my balls again."

She shook her head, her breathing getting more erratic as her clit got more and more sensitive. "No, I won't. You will call me Princess and I will think about you and me like this, and I will want to fuck you. Again."

"I could try and call you Becca, I suppose."

She stopped and opened her eyes wide, staring down at me. "Don't you dare. A change that big will scream, 'they're fucking'!"

The conversation was senseless and I smiled at her even though uncertainty was creeping in. We didn't have time for a serious talk. We would be fine as long as we kept ourselves professional. All I cared about was giving her one more thing to think about when I called her Princess.

"Lift up," I tapped her thigh, then pushed my fingers into her thin panties. Ripping them apart, I made a hole for my cock and lined up to her, shaking with anticipation.

"You owe me new panties," she smirked as she lowered herself on top of me.

"I'll give you the world, Princess. Whatever you want."

"Just make sure this is worth it Chase. Make it so that when I walk away from spring training without a job, I have no regrets."

Fuck, what was she asking for? Forever? Or an orgasm so good that nothing else mattered?

The idea of giving her both didn't scare me as much as I thought it would, but I settled for fucking her so hard she'd be walking with a limb and filling her up so much her work khakis would be stained with my cum.

"You want to go out again tonight?" Kace asked as we changed out of our uniforms after the game. "Ali wants to ask a friend to dinner again, so it's just us guys."

"Not tonight, man, I'm going to go to bed early." That wasn't a lie. I was going to be in Becca's bed so I faked a tired stretch, just to lay it on thick.

Becca and I had somehow managed to make it all day without seeing much of each other. That was both a blessing and a curse.

I missed her.

That morning, after I flipped her over and fucked her from behind, we made a deal. Try not to speak to each other all day, meet up for my work-out that evening, and fuck in her bed all night to make up for being so good all day.

It was a solid plan.

Kace's face morphed into a puzzled stare, and his eyes got darker the longer he stayed there. He started to speak, but the door swung open, and Fernandez called for me, making him stop and shut his mouth with a bite.

Instead of a conversation, Kace and I had a minute-long stare-down. He was obviously troubled by something, and I was confused, but whatever was bothering him wasn't something he wanted to discuss in front of Fernandez.

"Cap? I need Turner," Manny finally interrupted.

"He's all yours," Kace shrugged, still holding my eyes with his.

"Um…." Fernandez wasn't sure what to do so without finishing his sentence, he left and waited for me to follow.

"You okay, Cap?" I asked. One second, he was inviting me for drinks; the next, he was looking at me with disdain.

"Yep. Go see what Manny needs and I'll catch up with you later." His words seemed calmer than his stance. He started to back away, but I could tell something was still bothering him.

A million things ran through my mind as I tried to figure him out. All I did was tell him no to his invitation, which wasn't a first. So it had to be something else.

What the fuck, Cap?

becca

It had been a long day and I was exhausted from running between Eddie and Ethan. Pitchers were way needier than catchers. Then, I had a ton of paperwork and had to help one of the other interns with a chest wrap before the game started. The day has passed and I barely seen Chase at all.

The only time was in passing when I heard him and Fernandez discussing how they could help one of the pitchers with pitch signs after the game. I didn't pay much attention to their words, just Chase's ass in his dirty, played-in uniform, thinking of how he wrapped my legs around his waist and pushed into my body. The thought alone nearly had me weak for him all over again.

By some miracle, I got through the day without insisting he give me a striptease with his catcher's gear again. One little lie and I could have found an excuse to take him off the field and somewhere private so he could make me come. Resisting those ideas showed me I was stronger than I thought, but once the day was over, I wanted to curl up in his arms again.

Toward the end of the day, Ali called to ask me to have dinner with her again, but I turned her down, letting her know I was headed to bed early. Which wasn't a lie. Then she told me she was tired as well, and was going to insist the guys go out without her so she could rest as well.

Which was why when I heard the door open to the training room, where I was waiting for Chase later that night, I was surprised to see Kace in the doorway instead.

"Oh hey," I smiled, trying to play off my shock. "What are you doing here? I was just leaving."

"Just checking in," he said quietly, crossing his arms and legs and leaning on the door frame.

"Oh? Well, I'm fine. Just finishing up some things."

"Like what?" *Oh shit.* He was suspicious. He was questioning me. But I quickly remembered that I didn't owe him an answer.

"Work."

"Hmmmm."

"Aren't you supposed to be somewhere else?"

"Yeah well," he shoved off the door and walked further into the room. "I started thinking. Something isn't right, Becs."

He knew. But the lies had gotten so out of hand I didn't know which one he figured out. Just like with Gary, I panicked, unsure which direction our conversation was going in.

"Enlighten me," I shrugged nonchalantly, hoping he gave me a hint as to which lie he was busting me on.

"It's Chase, Becs. He hasn't been acting right."

"What does that have to do with me?" *Fuck.*

"You've been working closely with him, so I think you know what I mean."

"I have no idea what you're talking about," I practically yelled. If he thought I would implicate myself, he thought wrong. He was going to have to work harder to get the truth out of me.

"We need to talk this out. This is crazy shit, Becs."

"Stop acting like everything is your business."

"Well, this is *actually* my business."

I still wasn't sure how much he knew, but I was certain it

wasn't his business. In fact, I wasn't even going to satisfy him with a response.

Forget this. Forget him.

Chase would have to go a third night without his therapy because I wasn't going to hang around the stadium and subject myself to Kace's vague bullshit. As I stomped out and headed for the door, Kace mumbled behind me, "Don't ruin your career for him. Don't get yourself in trouble."

I winced at his words but kept moving forward. Chase was running behind, trying to grab our dinner, so I grabbed my phone and text him to give him a warning that there were players still at the field.

Who the hell was there this late?

> I didn't go in and find out. I just heard them using the equipment and left.

You want to come up to my room?

> Can you come to mine?

Of course, Princess. I'll bring food.

I lied again. It's what I did. But telling him the truth would have burst our bubble and I wasn't ready for that yet. If I was going to blow my career to pieces, I was going to have quite a few more Chase-induced orgasms first. That way, I would be too high to care. Plus, I was hoping that once I got a chance, I could explain things to Kace and beg him to keep quiet. At least until the end of spring training, because then I would be going home anyway.

Right?

When Chase got up to my room, I told him how I felt and he shut me down quickly.

"Princess, there isn't a chance in hell they're not hiring you for the season. They put Ethan and Eddie's treatment in your hands. That's a big deal."

Chewing the salad Chase had gotten me, I shook my head until I could swallow and speak. "I don't think so. I've been too much of a distraction for the team."

"Like what?"

I didn't answer with words, just used my fork to point to the knot still resting on my head.

"That was a freak thing and wasn't your fault," he scoffed.

"Would it have happened to one of the other guys? No. And," I added, "let's not forget, I'm also the reason you punched Manny."

"No," Chase mimicked me. "Fernandez got himself punched for being a dick."

"Whatever, I was the root cause."

"No," he said again, only with more conviction.

My appetite was gone and Instead of continuing to wallow in self-pity, I set my fork down and climbed onto Chase's lap. While he finished his dinner, I ran my nose along his neck.

"You're done eating?" He laughed quietly, holding onto my waist with one hand while taking another bite with his other.

"Doesn't taste as good as you do," I teased.

"How about," he pushed me back and looked into my eyes. "While I finish my dinner, you strip down and lay on the bed."

His words made me nervous, but I slid off his lap and onto my knees on the floor. His eyes heated and I realized no matter what I did, he would think it was hot. He seemed to think everything I did was sexy.

Staying on the floor, I crawled toward the bed and shook my ass as much as I could. My standard issued khakis weren't very attractive, but making him want me despite their drab look was part of the fun.

Turning back to face him, I lifted up and pulled my shirt over my head, tossing it toward him as I shook my hair out. Before working on my pants, I flicked the back of my bra open and let it slide down my arms. He hummed as he took another bite of his food and I could tell he was trying to stay put and let me finish.

My nipples were hard and I pushed my tits together, flicking them with my thumbs and teasing him. "I love it when you touch me here."

"Fuck," he whispered under his breath, moving in his seat a little.

When I stood up, I flicked my pants open and pushed my hand into my panties, feeling how wet I was before I let him see me. Running a finger through my folds, I pulled it out and painted my bottom lip with it, hoping it looked as sexy as it felt.

His cock was hard, and he adjusted himself as he dropped the fork onto his plate.

"You're done eating?" I asked, using his same words.

"Done with my dinner," he smiled. "Now time for dessert."

I started to roll my eyes at his cheesy line, but his face was hard and his eyes were focused. He stood up quickly and lifted me by the thighs before dropping me onto the bed. My pants were brought down with force and he ripped my delicate panties from my body. Pushing my legs wide, he locked his eyes with mine and ran his tongue up my clit. His moan made it sound as if he was eating a delicacy and I trembled beneath him.

He continued to taste me, flicking his tongue over every sensitive part of me, and sucking on my clit until my whole body was shaking. Then he would stop and watch as I settled back down before diving back in to tease me again.

"Stop," I cried. "Please."

"I love you on edge," he growled against my clit. "I love…"

He never got to finish before my body let go, making him wrap his lips around me and push his tongue inside of me, tasting everything he was eliciting from my body. Before I was completely down from the high, I heard him shuffling his shorts down and felt him pushing inside of me.

I practically screamed as I started to tense again. My legs

wrapped around his waist and I held onto his shoulders as he thrusted in and out of me. It was a good thing we were in my room, because I was so loud, I knew the neighbors in the hotel would be able to hear me. If we were in his room, Kace would be able to hear and he would know I was being fucked.

"Chase!"

"Come again, Cupcake. Come for me so I can feel you squeezing my cock."

My heart was beating out of my chest and tears started forming in my eyes. The emotions I felt as he fucked me harder and harder was messing with my head. It was making me wonder what he was about to say before I came. It made me wonder if he was feeling as much for me as I was for him.

Pretending for a minute that he did, my body reacted and I started pulsing around him, just like he wanted me to. He bit his lip, trying to keep himself quiet, but the look in his eyes told me how much he loved what he was feeling.

When he motions got jerky, and his body slowed down, he fell on top of me and nuzzled his nose into my ear. His breathing was harsh, but as it softened and slowed down, I realized I could lay there forever with him inside of me. It was the most content feeling I had ever known and once he moved, it felt like it would all go away.

Eventually, he shifted and laid next to me, both of us refusing to get up as we laid together in the mess we made. It was too quiet, though, and my thoughts started making my heart race once again.

"Chase?"

"Yeah, Princess?"

"What is this?" I didn't really know what I was asking and the answer scared me, but it was all I had running through my head.

"I don't know. But I like it."

"Me too," I smiled, happy that he was as confused as me.

chase

SPRING TRAINING WAS SAILING BY AND I WAS HAVING MY BEST START of my career with six home runs in five days. Coincidently, it had been five days since Becca and I stopped fighting each other and I fucked her against the right field wall. Since that night, we had spent every other night in each other's bed.

When we were at the stadium, we kept ourselves professional. It wasn't as hard as I thought it was going to be because it was kind of fun. When we were alone at the end of the day, we laughed about the little things that happened.

"Your face when Eddie started explaining his toe fungus almost had me losing it."

"I was trying to stay professional, but I almost begged you to carry me away."

"I would have saved you."

All Becca had to do was say the word, and I would save her from anything. Not that she needed to be saved. My girl was strong and confident. She always told me how nervous she was on the field, or talking to certain people, but it didn't show.

On top of being a beautiful badass, she was brilliant. Her intelligence shone as I watched her work. Her level of knowledge, and ability to reason through a problem amazed me. I knew I was seeing her differently as we got closer, but I didn't doubt everyone else could see that she belonged there. The team would be better with her around, and she would be offered that position for full time. I knew she would.

Then she and I would have some decisions to make. Spring training was one thing, but when the season started, it was grueling and long. It was still fun, but way more serious, and if we continued whatever it was that we had, it wouldn't be long before we got caught. The smartest thing I could have done was cut ties before we got too serious, then step back and watch her shine from afar.

But I didn't.

I wouldn't.

I couldn't.

I was too happy and too selfish. We had eight days before spring training ended. Eight days to see each other, be with each other and soak each other in before we had to walk away. I wasn't going to waste it being noble.

Despite how much Becca denied it, I was convinced Kace knew about us. He didn't speak to me, didn't invite me out anymore, and eyed me like he was waiting for me to kill an innocent puppy or something.

I couldn't figure out why he would care, except that none of us, including Kace, wanted to see Becca raked through the coals for her affair with a player. It would be safe to assume he didn't think I cared about Becca, and was just using her for a warm body, not considering the risks she was taking.

Whatever his problem was, he was staying quiet. But I knew

he would do what any team captain would do, and in eight days he would level with me and tell me whatever he needed to.

Until then, I was focusing on Fernandez's latest bullshit.

"We need to dumb down the signs for Keith, man. He just isn't getting it."

Keith Sanders was a relief pitcher, new to the team. New to the league. When I put down one finger for a fastball, he threw a changeup. He could pitch his ass off, but Manny wasn't wrong. Keith struggled with the signs.

"How much simpler can it get?" I asked, looking at the other two catchers for their opinion.

We had huddled up in a conference room for a catcher's meeting, and Keith was the main topic. When no one replied, Manny sighed and hit his fist on the table.

"Okay, then let's talk about why he's so dumb." I started to roll my eyes at how he blatantly called another teammate "dumb." But his following words made me spit my water across the table before my eyes had a chance to do anything. "He's fucking the intern."

"What the fuck?"

"I'm just calling it as I see it."

"What did you see?"

"Keith on the phone, saying he was 'headed up to the intern's room for another quick fuck.'"

"That's impossible." *Wasn't it?*

"It's not impossible." *It had to be.* "Those were his exact words. And he didn't know I was listening, so he had no reason to lie. Just fucking talk to him. Tell him to get his head in the damn game. You take the lead on this. That's your job."

I was nodding but in complete disbelief. Fernandez had to be mistaken. Becca was a lot of things, but she wasn't promiscuous.

Was she?

Fuck! I hated even questioning her based on one sentence from Fernandez. He dropped that bomb and then walked out of the room, telling us he needed to piss. The other guys followed him out, over the whole topic, and I was alone in that conference room for God knows how long, trying to piece the information together.

I didn't have a right to hold Becca to a monogamous relationship when we never discussed it. I could acknowledge that. But that made me think that if it bothered me so much, maybe we needed to have that discussion. In that moment, I realized that just fucking her wasn't working for me. I wanted more, even if it was only for eight days.

Nothing we discussed, or did together, indicated she was with anyone else but me. Hell, she had battled herself and her feelings since day one, trying not to lose her grasp on her job. Sure, she blew that to fucking hell when we finally surrendered to one another. But I was convinced that we were the exception.

We were worth it.

We were inevitable.

So, it didn't feel as wrong as it would if she were with someone else, much less more than one person.

After a while, I stood from the table, knowing I had to get to work but still with no idea how I would handle everything. All I knew was I wasn't talking to Keith until I talked to Becca. I may have been pissed, but I cared too much about her to not speak with her first.

She was going to be so pissed when I mentioned that the news came from Manny Fernandez. I could practically see her ears steaming.

Then I stopped in the doorway, halting abruptly. Turning back to face the empty room like it held a secret code, I looked around, my thoughts all coming together in a wave of relief and sanity.

It was right then that I knew in my gut Fernandez was lying.

He hated Becca.

He hated what she did to him.

He hated that I punched him for her.

He hated that she ended up being right.

He was lying and was probably trying to discredit her.

Keith was a good fall guy. He was distracted, but he wouldn't get in trouble. He was too low on the totem pole for the suits in the front office to worry about.

Becca would be ruined.

Fernandez chose to tell *me* for a reason. He wanted me to be the one to blow the whistle and give Becca a reason to hate me after I punched his face for calling her a bitch. What he didn't know was that since that day, Becca had buried herself in my life way deeper than my need to defend her honor over name-calling. I was in so deep with her that I would stop at nothing to see to it that Manny Fernandez never played another game with my team again if he so much as looked at her the wrong way.

In the meantime, I wouldn't give him the satisfaction of upsetting Becca. She didn't need to know what Fernandez was accusing her of. She didn't need his bullshit at the forefront of her mind.

The thought that it may spook her into cutting things off with me flitted through my head as well, and I wasn't proud of it, but I would be lying if I said that wasn't another reason I would be keeping it to myself.

becca

"CHASE? WHERE ARE WE GOING?"

"You know I like to surprise you." He winked and shifted gears as he sped up onto the interstate.

"Disney World again?" I guessed, even though we weren't headed in that direction.

He silently shook his head no.

We were down to seven days before spring training ended, making me happy and sad at the same time. The whole experience had been harder than I anticipated, but more rewarding than I could have imagined.

Chase and I had talked about it briefly, and both came to opposite conclusions; he thought I would be hired on for the season, and I thought there was no way in hell that was happening. But for the most part, we didn't talk about work.

After we finished his therapy and showered, he told me to get dressed because he wanted to take me somewhere. I snuck down to the parking garage and once we were on the road, I felt free. It was easy to pretend we were regular people going on a date. Disney didn't count. So much had changed between us since then.

When Chase wasn't shifting the car, his hand was in mine. His sexy forearm rested on my thigh, and I held onto it with the hand he wasn't holding. I gently brushed the soft skin on the inside of his arm, causing goosebumps to form every so often. He turned and smiled at me, sometimes lifting my hand to his lips and kissing my knuckles.

Everything was different.

Better.

Scarier.

It worried me, that in seven days, when we had to return to the real world, I wouldn't be able to walk away from him. We hadn't discussed what we were or what we wanted yet. What we had right then seemed to be the only important thing.

My thoughts kept me busy and I lost track of time as I looked out the window as the car. Not until we slowed into a big, empty parking lot did I start to wonder where we were.

Chase parked and made his way to my side of the car, helping me out, keeping my hand tightly in his. I could hear the sound of the ocean and the waves breaking in the background and I smiled as I realized where we were.

"The beach," I whispered.

"The beach," he repeated with a smile.

He led me to the edge of the parking lot, where a boardwalk started and led out onto the sand. We were only five steps on the boardwalk when the ocean came into view. The moon shone over the water, giving us the only light for miles. It was not the first time I had seen the ocean, but it was the first time I had seen it at night, hand in hand with a man.

I was a little nervous and hoped, for just two seconds, that Chase wasn't a serial killer. But if I had to die, it wouldn't be the worst way to go. That thought was fleeting, and I laughed at myself.

"What's so funny?"

"Just thinking how this is a great place to murder someone. You're not a serial killer, right?"

Chase smirked at my blunt response and shook his head. "I guess I should be thankful you're considering your safety, since keeping you safe has suddenly become vital to my sanity. Since seeing that ball hit your head, I have been insane every time your feet touch that field during a game."

Waving him off, I tried to downplay what he was saying, but I knew it was true. Every time I walked to the mound to talk to Ethan or Eddie, his eyes followed me with a protective gleam. When I went to help one of them stretch down the foul line, he worried.

But that wasn't going to happen again. Security was aware that they had to be wary of fans throwing baseballs at employees on the field. Not to mention, most fans were amazing. I wasn't going to let the actions of a jealous few scare me into thinking that would happen again.

We continued walking to the end of the boardwalk and slipped our flip-flops off before stepping onto the soft white sand. We walked to the edge and let the cool water ebb and flow onto our feet. Our walk was silent for a while, and I used that time to let my mind wander again. What could Chase and I have outside of Florida? Outside of hiding and lying?

I daydreamed about seeing each other in public, holding hands, and telling everyone we were together. I imagined telling my family, and bringing him home to meet them. I even imagined my brother being happy for us. Which was a pipe dream because Cam would hate me dating a baseball player, especially one he considered a friend.

"Do you like kids?" Chase asked out of the blue.

Random questions were how I found out he loves to cook, believes in aliens, and doesn't dance. But as time went on, they were getting deeper and I didn't want to get too deep and ruin the mood, especially with the uncertainties of our future. So, I answered his question and asked another question, hoping to change the subject.

"I like kids, they're funny. Are you superstitious?"

He eyed me knowingly and smiled. But ultimately, he let me change the subject.

"Isn't every baseball player superstitious to some degree?"

"I see Ethan do a tap dance with his toe several times before he takes the field each inning. Eddie only lets me wrap his wrists clockwise. Kris plays the same song three times every morning before walking to the field. Manny takes some secret vitamin every morning. Kace…."

"Wait. Fernandez does what?"

I blinked, thrown off for a minute by Chase's abrupt interruption.

"What?" I asked, unsure what part he had trouble with.

"Fernandez does what?" he repeated calmly.

"I saw him taking some pills when I first started. He told me they were vitamins and more for his superstition than anything."

"Vitamins?"

"That's what he said."

"Princess, the odds of Fernandez taking 'vitamins' because of superstition is well below zero. Keep an eye on him. No, wait. I'll keep an eye on him."

"Oh shit," I muttered, feeling slightly guilty for believing Manny so easily. There was a chance Chase was wrong, too, but I decided I would be keeping an eye on him either way.

Chase pulled my hand and continued our walk, shrugging off the errant way our conversation trailed and picked up right where we left off. "I have a few superstitions. They vary to some degree. When I'm hitting good, I try to keep up the same routines. When I'm in a slump, I do a different set of things. It all depends."

"You've been raking these past few weeks."

He squeezed my hand and winked at me. "I have also been keeping my same routine."

Ever since he had me up against that right field wall, he'd been hitting baseballs over that wall every chance he got. His catching game had been on point as well. Not to mention, he hadn't complained of knee pain in a while. Of course, I chalked that up to the work we had been doing and not so much how many times we'd been in bed together. Or against a wall. Or in the shower.

"Just doing my part to help the team," I joked, getting a small laugh from Chase.

We walked in the moonlight a little farther, conversation flowing smoothly. Once we went so far, we turned around and walked back. It was such a simple night, but I felt like it was the most monumental thing I had ever done. We were solidifying a connection we knew would break in a few days.

As amazing as it was, spending all our time in bed didn't feel natural. I wanted to eat with him, walk with him, laugh with him, talk with him. He was making all the risks and lies worth it.

I was scared, but I couldn't stop.

Besides, I knew I wouldn't get the long-term job with the trouble my presence had caused all spring. Being with Chase was my solace—not my goal when I got there, but something that made the time away worth it.

Once we returned to the parking lot near the car, Chase stopped our walk. He faced me, holding both hands as he looked down at me. I smiled up at him, quiet and waiting for whatever was floating through his mind to surface to his lips.

"How is it I don't even know your last name?" He smiled at the question, but I was sure I went pale.

At that point, I should have told him. I promised myself that I would be honest if I was ever asked. But until that moment, no one had. As close as Chase and I had gotten, it was a natural question. And if we were any other people, I would tell him. But would he connect me to Cam? And how would knowing who my brother was affect our next seven days? Would he be mad?

Cam had been around for the last week and a half, coming to games and hanging with the guys in the evenings. Apart from the one night Chase went out with them, he had been making lame excuses not to join them. Instead, he was spending all his time with me. But I knew he thought the world of Cam—he had said so in one of our many conversations. Which was, of course, another subject I had changed quickly.

"Because you've insisted on calling me Princess, or Cupcake, or… what was it? Lady Goliath? Crazy Kingkiller?" I was deflecting, smiling, and hoping he forgot to ask again.

"Well, I'm not wrong. You are a Kingkiller." He pointed to himself, "I'm an Atlanta King, and you're killing me."

I barked a laugh at his lame joke but smiled at his charm. I was also pleased with how well I had deflected so I kept talking.

"Well," I started swinging our intertwined hands and looking up at him, "Mr. Atlanta King, this has been the best night. There's just one thing missing."

He raised an eyebrow in question. Nothing was missing; it was the perfect way to spend time with him. But I needed to continue distracting him from his question.

"If only you knew how to dance," I joked.

He smiled and looked up to the sky. "Okay, I see what you're trying to do here."

Wait? Did he?

When he looked back down at me, his gaze was part cockiness and part mischief. He let go of one of my hands and reached into his pocket. He thumbed his phone for a minute before setting it onto the hood of his car.

When he took my hand back, he placed it on his shoulder and then put his hand on my back. We were poised for a slow dance just as the music started playing. He pulled me closer, his mouth to my ear and his breath a whisper, "I said I *didn't* dance, not that I couldn't."

We stared, swaying in time to the soft country song he had turned on. Ironically, the song was about slow dancing in a parking lot making the moment even more amazing.

As the song ended, our soft sway did as well and I pushed up on my tiptoes, whispering against his lips, "Your secret is safe with me."

chase

In thirty-three years, I had never wanted an actual, exclusive relationship. But in only a matter of weeks, I could no longer stand the thought of not being with Becca. As scary as that was, though, I was ready for it. I didn't plan on her. There was no way I could have seen it coming, even when I spotted her in the lobby that first day. Initially, I couldn't see having her in my life past a few nights in my bed.

Now I just wanted her all the time. Everywhere.

Not shouting it from the rooftops was harder than I thought it would be. I had to stop myself from running through the locker room and shouting, "Mine," every time Becca walked by. I was even close to having a jacket made for her that said Property of Chase Turner on the back. Or maybe some stickers. Fuck, I could have put stickers on everything.

The secrecy of our relationship had me thinking of wild ways to claim her when all I really wanted was to just turn to Kris or Ethan and say, "Hey man, Becca's my girl."

As long as we were both working for the Kings, though, that couldn't happen. And I would never ask her to compromise her career and dreams for me.

Which brought me back to my initial thought: How long could I keep hiding my feelings about her? How long could we make it work? Was talking about an actual relationship even worth it?

Sitting at my locker, preparing for the game, I was deep in a daydream when my phone rang, snapping me out of it.

"Yeah?" I answered, still slightly in my head with Becca.

"Chase, good news, man!" It was my agent, Tim. He didn't call me much, so I perked up instantly at his words.

"I need some good news. What's up?"

"I'm getting on a plane tomorrow and headed to Florida. The Kings want to negotiate that big contract before the season starts next week."

"What?" I stood from my stool in shock. "That wasn't supposed to happen until next year."

"I've only caught a few of the televised games so far, but you've been playing better than I have ever seen you play. I guess they see it too and want to lock you down."

That news was the best-case scenario in terms of my future. It meant I didn't have to get through another year with my knees. I just had to get through the next few days. Once the contract was signed, I could scale back and rest the way I should have been doing all along. Which would make Becca happy, and I was suddenly antsy to tell her.

My confession to her was true. It wasn't all about the money, but a lucrative contract stood for everything I had worked for since I was twelve years old and decided I wanted to play Major League Baseball.

It meant respect. It meant a longer career.

It also meant avoiding my dad a bit longer.

"They're signing you a year early?" Becca jumped up and down on my bed in excitement. "Thank God!"

"You seem a little more invested than just being happy for me," I joked.

"Hell yeah, I am. I'm happy for *me* and all the other Kings' fans. We don't need Fernandez behind the plate full time. He'd drive us, and the pitching staff, right into the bottom of the division."

When she showed up for dinner in my room, I couldn't wait to tell her about my call from Tim. But I hadn't realized she would be so fervent. It made my heart swell even more.

Grabbing her hand, I pulled her off her feet and onto my lap. She curled into me like she had been doing it for years, with each of her legs wrapped around my waist, and her arms around my neck.

"I'm glad you're glad, Princess," I spoke into her lips before kissing her with a soft peck.

"I'm so happy for you, Pancake. I know how much this means to you." Her nickname made me melt a little as she kissed me again, that time more passionately.

Within a few seconds, she was moving her hip and grinding on my body. She was going to kill me with her need, so flipped her onto her back and made quick work of her khakis and t-shirt. Burying my cock between her legs, I looked down at her as I gave her all I had.

I knew her body, and I knew it well. So, it wasn't long before she screamed my name and begged me for more while simultaneously trying to tear the rest of my clothes off. Seeing her in her element at work was sexy, but seeing her needy for me and demanding my cock was the target I lived for.

I could easily fuck her every damn day for the rest of my life.

For thirty-three years, I assumed having a relationship with a woman would be a downfall—a distraction. Now, I realized that I had just never met a woman worth the risk.

Becca was worth it. We proved that every day when we snuck in and out of each other's rooms, when we caught a glance of each other across the locker room, when we sucked in a quiet breath every time we touched in the training room.

As it turned out, Becca wasn't much of a distraction at all. She was my savior and my new lucky charm.

My world.

becca

"How is it I have been down here for almost two weeks, and you and I have only hung out twice now?" Ali asked as we laid in her hotel room, eating greasy cheese fries and drinking wine.

I shrugged, but I wasn't sure she could see me since we were both looking at the ceiling. "I have been so busy. This job is every day, all the time."

It wasn't far from the truth, but I wasn't ready to tell her I spent my downtime with Chase. A few more days, and I would no longer be working for the team. I knew I would tell her then —maybe.

"Well, at least we have tonight!"

We didn't have much planned. Just hanging out in her room, a little girl- talk, and having wine. Cam and Kace were hanging out again with some of the guys from the team again, and that included Chase.

As far as I knew, Kace had decided to let his suspicions with Chase go, since he hadn't said anything to him or me. Or anyone else for that matter. Cam was still his usual, happy self, and Ali would have hounded me for details if she knew.

When Chase told me the guys invited him out, I encouraged

him to go. He normally would have if it wasn't for me, and it seemed suspicious that he was always turning them down. Plus, I needed time with Ali before she became suspicious of me. And Chase didn't know yet that I was close to her.

A few more days, Becca.

If my head didn't explode before the end of the week, I would be okay and could explain things to Chase, Then I could tell my brother how I felt about Chase, and apply for jobs back in the high school circuit—where I was safe from falling for the players.

As I sat up to refill my wine, Ali followed and held up her glass.

"Whatever happened to Isla?" She was ready for the real talk, but I was ready to close that embarrassing story for good.

"Nothing. The guy went back to be with her, and I haven't seen him since."

"She was a girlfriend? He was down here in Florida cheating on her? What a pig, you're better off."

"Yep," I popped, and brought the wine to my lips.

Before I took a sip, I paused because something didn't feel right. My stomach had been in knots all day, and I was on the verge of getting sick. It was either the greasy fries, or the mounting lies.

Setting my glass of wine down, I held my stomach and hoped it settled down. But after another rumble, I lurched forward and ran toward the bathroom, immediately throwing up the entire contents of our girls' night.

Oh my God!

"Are you okay?" Ali came running in behind me.

"Yes." *No.* I waved her off, tucking my head into my hands and praying for peace. Or death. Ali handed me a wet washcloth and backed away, giving me a minute to collect myself.

When I slowly moved back into the main room, Ali stood up and threw her hands around. "Becs, what the hell?"

"I think it was the grease," I mumbled. "Or the wine."

"We barely made a dent in the wine."

"Maybe I'm getting sick. I'm going to lay down in my room. I'm sorry."

"Girl, yes, go lay down."

When I started gathering my things, I was careful not to move too quickly. I felt triggered, like one false move would make me throw up again.

Ali hugged me goodbye, but then held onto my shoulders and leveled her eyes to mine. "Can I just ask one question?"

"What?"

"There isn't a chance you're pregnant is there?"

My eyes widened, I started to shake my head no, but the movement was too much and her words were making my stomach churn again. I ran into the bathroom and shut myself in with a slam of the door.

Pregnant?

"Becs? You okay? I hope I didn't freak you out. I just kind of wondered. You saw that guy a few weeks ago, and I wouldn't blame you if you two hooked up. And now, all of a sudden, you're sick. I mean, it could totally be the flu, or definitely the grease, like you said. Yeah, that's probably it…" Ali was rambling, and I was too weak to stop her. "But when a girl gets sick and craves greasy fries all of a sudden… It's okay to be pregnant. You are crazily loved. It's okay!"

"Pregnant?" I heard a thunderous male voice.

Cam.

"Pregnant?" That sounded like Kace.

"Baby, are you pregnant?" Cam went from sounding confused to excited in a matter of seconds, which made almost made me giggle despite how awful I felt.

Meanwhile, Ali chose that moment to stop talking altogether. She was probably debating what was safer letting them think she was pregnant, or confessing that she thought I was.

"Becs is in the bathroom," Ali finally said quietly.

"So, you're not in here giving yourself a pep talk about being pregnant?" Kace almost sounding sad. They must have walked in at the end of her speech.

Did they want Ali to get pregnant?

Shit, I had a ton of questions. But none of those could be answered in that moment. I needed to get the hell out of there before I vomited again.

As I splashed water on my face, reality dawned on the guys.

"You mean Becs is pregnant?" Cam yelled.

I swayed, trying to open the door but failing, feeling weak and exhausted.

"No, maybe," Ali answered. "Becca was seeing a guy here in town a few weeks ago. He left town and ended up having a girl-friend. She was pretty upset if you remember. I'm pretty sure they hooked up. Now she is craving greasy fries and throwing up."

"She was seeing someone. How did she have time for that?" Kace asked, sounding immediately suspicious.

"I don't know. But he's gone home now. He was just here for a few days."

The good news was Ali's story threw Kace off the scent of me and Chase. The bad news was, I was too sick to even care if they thought I was pregnant. I didn't have the strength to correct them. All I wanted was to run as far away as possible.

The door to the hallway was close by the bathroom door, so when I cracked it open, I made a run for it and prayed I got to my room before I got sick again.

I made it to my room without any more vomit.

I even managed to brush my teeth and return a text from Ali, assuring her I was fine once she realized I ran out of the door.

Chase also texted me and wanted to come to my room since his night was over, but I didn't want him to see me the way I was. Not that it mattered much. When I told him I wasn't feeling well, he showed up anyway with chicken soup and carrot cake.

I couldn't eat it.

But we laid together, and I fell asleep in his arms as his fingers ran through my hair.

I was glad he didn't listen to me and came anyway. I needed him there with me to feel content and comfortable.

The following day, I woke up feeling a little queasy but much better than the night before.

Chase was already on the floor doing his stretches without me, with headphones in. He hadn't realized I was awake yet so I stared for a minute.

He leaned in on his bent left knee, with his right leg stretched to the side. The muscles in his side rippled as he pulsed in the stretch. Then he leaned over and did the other side. I stayed as still as possible, enjoying how his sweatpants hung low on his waist. I could tell he hadn't bothered with anything under those pants.

My heart swelled, thinking of how far we had come in the past few weeks. It wasn't that we were ever enemies, but we sure as hell hadn't made life easy on one another. All of that initial friction had disappeared the second we finally gave in to one another—physically, emotionally, even professionally.

I knew I had failed myself when it came to the job. I had lost sight of everything I set out to do while I was there, and broke all the rules.

I became a distraction.

I fell for a player.

But I didn't regret it.

No matter how many more years I spent at the high school

level, or how it all ended with Chase, I would never regret feeling the way he made me feel.

"Morning, Princess." Chase had turned and realized my eyes were open.

"Don't stop," I moaned. "Keep going. In fact, lose the sweatpants and stretch naked."

"Enjoying the show?"

"I would enjoy it more if you were naked."

"Well, as much as I want to indulge your every fantasy, Princess, I have to get to the stadium."

He leaned in and kissed my nose. An intimate gesture that made my heart want to burst. I started to get up, too, hoping I would feel better after a shower, but Chase held me down.

"Where're you going?"

"Work?" *Wasn't it obvious?*

"Cupcake, you need to chill. Just for a day."

"I'm fine, Chase. It was just something I ate."

"Yeah, that's probably true, but why not just take one day off to be sure?"

"I can't afford to do that. I have too much work to do. Plus, Eddie is starting today. I'll feel guilty if I am not on the bench."

"Gary can handle it. But if you really are sick, and go in and get us all sick, then you're gonna feel worse."

Dammit. He had a point. Although I felt better, I didn't feel one hundred percent, so I needed to do what was best for the team and hang tight until I was sure I was okay.

"Fine," I conceded. "I'll text Gary and tell him I was sick last night and probably need twenty-four hours to get right."

"Good girl," he said, kissing my forehead. "The game is televised today, so you can keep an eye on Eddie from right here in your bed."

"If I'm in bed, Eddie isn't the one I'll be keeping my eyes on," I teased.

"Maybe I need to send you a special message today. Like every time I think about you, I will wiggle my fingers before I give Eddie the sign."

I smiled so big my face hurt and leaned to kiss Chase on his neck. "Well, I'll be watching closely," I murmured against his skin. "The TV camera angle is perfect when you're crushing on the catcher."

"Is that so?" he smiled, enjoying my tease.

"Yep. Direct shot. Right between the legs."

chase

I WIGGLED MY FINGERS SO MANY TIMES EDDIE THOUGHT I HAD A cramp. Eventually, I had to walk to the mound and tell him to deal with it because my fingers were wiggling all day. I just couldn't stop thinking about Becca, and knowing she was watching made me want to show her how much I thought about her.

Even as I crouched behind the plate, warming up a relief pitcher coming into the game, Becca was all I could think about. I couldn't wait to get back to her and make sure she was okay. When I left, she looked better than the night before, but what if she needed me?

After I got through a few more innings, I left the game to let Fernandez get some innings in. Since Becca had mentioned his vitamins, I had been watching him, and there wasn't a doubt in my mind that the "vitamin" he took caused his balls to shrink. I just hadn't seen him take them yet.

Even if I did see him take them, I probably needed to let it play out naturally without being a tattletale. But that wouldn't happen either. Fernandez shot himself in the foot where Becca was concerned. He had it out for her, and I would do anything to protect her.

Sitting at my locker, I checked my phone and sighed in relief when I got the two routine texts from Isla telling me that my dad was okay. Then there were two texts from Tim letting me know how the meetings were going, and that I would be brought in with an offer the next day. Lastly, I had one beautiful text from Becca. A picture of her kissing me on the TV as I went up to bat in the 3rd inning with the caption.

You must be thinking about me a lot today. ;-)

Damn, I loved that woman.

No slip of the mind, no bullshit, no freak-out realization. I sincerely loved her.

What else did it mean when she was all I thought about? When I wanted her to be happier than anyone in the world, and I wanted to be the reason she smiled every day?

As scary as our future was—particularly the next few days— loving her wasn't as scary as I had always thought love would be.

"Hey, Turner," Kace called me from the other side of the locker room. He had still been stiff with me but had obviously decided that whatever his beef was, he would deal with it later because he had dropped the glare he had been giving me and was using actual words again.

Yeah, Cap? What's up?"

"I heard your agent is in town. You ready for the dotted lines?"

"Yep. It's what I've been working so hard for."

He snorted and shook his head. "I'm going to let you do you, but you need to think long and hard about the impact this is going to have."

Snapping my head up to him, I had a million questions in my

eyes. What impact? It was my damn life. My career. My everything.

Besides her.

Kace put his hands up in surrender, not wanting it to be a more extensive discussion. "I want you behind that plate for this team. But I want you to be the best you can be while you're back there. If anything is holding you up… All I'm saying is you need to think long-term. I'm going to back off and let you be the veteran player I know you are, but just food for thought."

What in the actual fuck?

Kace walked off toward the showers, leaving me confused and irritated. How would being with Becca not be me "being my best self"? Hell, I had never been better since I met her—both on and off the field.

Long- term? Everything about her and I was long-term. We may not have had that talk yet, but it was inevitable. You didn't just walk away from something like us.

I skipped a shower and headed straight to the hotel—straight to Becca. She opened the door, looking much better than before I left. I kissed her cheek as I walked in and ran a hand down the curve of her hips.

"Good game," she smiled.

"It would have been better if you were there."

"I meant on the field. A double, an RBI, and you called a great game behind the plate. Not to mention all those extra signs you were throwing."

Laughing, I may have gone overboard on our secret code, but I really was thinking about her the whole time.

"Still would have been better if you were there." I walked farther into the room, taking stock of her room service spread and the rumpled sheets on the bed. "How're you feeling? Better?"

"Mmmhhhhmmmm," she nodded, looking a little blissed out. "Just really, really missed you." She rose to her tiptoes and kissed me, wrapping her hands around my neck.

I savored the taste of her minty lips—something I hadn't indulged in case she was super sick. She leaned in for more, rubbing her stomach along the front of my shorts, feeling for any hardness and friction.

It was there. Her lips did that to me. But I pulled back and stopped her. "I need a shower. I came right over here instead of showering."

"Me too," she whispered. "Let's do that together."

She didn't have to tell me twice, and the hardness she was previously looking for showed up with her words. I followed her like a puppy into the bathroom and watched her undress and turn the water on.

With the water raining down on us, she went down to her knees and looked up at me before slipping her tongue out to taste the tip of my cock. Even if she wasn't one-hundred percent better, I couldn't help grabbing her hair and forcing myself down her throat. Her gagging noises made me feel a little guilty, but when I tried to pull back, she bit down and shook her head, daring me to stop.

"You okay gagging on my cock, Baby?"

She hummed and nodded, swirling her tongue like I was a damn ice cream cone. My hands went to the tiled wall behind her and I slammed down trying to get myself under control. But my hips pumped into her mouth, her hands ran up my inner thigh, and when I was sure I was about to come, I tilted her head back and made sure everything I had ran right down her throat.

"That's it," I moaned. "You're mine. This mouth is mine."

She swallowed and popped her lips off the tip of me before standing up. Her tongue pushed into my mouth and I could taste my own saltiness as we warred for the upper hand.

My fingers traced a path down her body and when I found her core, I pushed inside of her, pumping in and out. Her tits bounced as we moved, and I felt her knees starting to give out. My cock was already hard again so I withdrew my fingers and pushed inside of her, holding her up between my body and the wall.

"I could stay here inside your pussy forever," I confessed. "You were made for me, Princess."

She sucked in a breath, but stayed quiet, aside from her moans of pleasure. Her arms wrapped around my shoulders and when she squeezed, I knew she was letting herself go. Her pussy held me tight and I exploded inside of her, loving the warmth of our combined releases against my skin.

As we tried to center ourselves again, and get cleaned up, we stayed quiet and smiled. No words were needed, even the ones I'd gone there to say in the first place. There was so much I wanted to talk to her about, but I no longer had the strength.

My conversation with Kace.

My contract negotiations.

My dad.

Life.

Us.

Everything.

becca

Gary greeted me the next day by smiling and asking me to come into the office. He was usually gruff and matter-of-fact, but he had somehow managed a smile that made me smile back.

"Morning, Becca! Come on in, come on in."

"Okay," I answered hesitantly. "Did I win the lottery?"

"Something like that."

Rising an eyebrow in confusion, I followed him into the office.

"We had meetings yesterday, and it was unanimously decided among the staff and coaches, to offer you the full-time position with the team this upcoming regular season."

My jaw dropped in shock, barely able to respond as he kept filling me in.

"We have been very impressed with you these last few weeks. You have been the epitome of professionalism despite everything that was thrown your way," he cleared his throat and added, "literally thrown your way."

I had no words.

"That includes knowing your limits and taking yesterday off

to make sure you were well enough to be around everyone. Little things like that go a long way in this business."

I still couldn't speak.

"We know some of the guys have been unruly, and haven't taken to a woman roaming the locker room, but you never let that stop you or get in your way," he continued. "We need someone like you on this team, someone that can put these guys in their place when it needs to be done. You up for the challenge?"

I started nodding, still in shock, then found my voice. "Can I be honest? I didn't see this coming. This isn't an attempt to reach an equal opportunity employer quota, is it?"

Shut up and say thank you, Becca!

Gary scoffed and shook his head. "I assure you, the big guys that pay the bills do not give a shit about equal opportunity employment. They only want the best. And from what we have all seen so far, you're the best."

I began pacing the room. It wasn't that I wasn't excited, I was ecstatic, but I had planned on *not* getting the job. Which meant I had gotten excited about moving forward with Chase.

There was no way we could make us work if I was there all season. We would be found out eventually. We were too close to parading each other around as it was. But were we in so deep that we couldn't call it off and still be friends? Could I work closely with him every day, knowing I couldn't have him?

Gary mistook my worry over Chase as concern for the job in general, so he spoke up to stop my pacing.

"Becca, this is a two-way street. If you have any concerns, you just have to ask. In the meantime, we won't sign anything for a day or two, so you have time to think this offer through."

I thanked him and then quietly carried my concerns with me for the rest of the day. I kept to myself as much as possible, weighing the decision on a constant loop inside my head.

By the end of the day, Chase must have decided enough was

enough because he pulled me into a janitorial closet in the hallway as we passed one another.

"Baby, you okay? You've looked pale all day. You still sick?"

I just nodded, not knowing which question I was answering exactly. I was too busy debating on whether I should tell him the truth. Should I just ask if he and I are forever? Was that too much, too soon, for him? I didn't want to scare him away.

"Gary offered me the job," I whispered.

In the dim light, I saw Chase's eyes light up with excitement. He scooped me into his arms and twirled me around the best he could in the confined space. "Congrats! This is what you wanted. You deserve it."

I nodded again, still low on my word count, considering the epic moment it was.

"Wait." Chase backed up and looked into my eyes. "You're happy, right?"

"I am. This is my dream job." Turning my back to him, I tried collecting the strength to finish my thoughts. When I turned back, a tear had escaped my eyes, falling down my cheek slowly. Chase's eyes followed the tear for a minute before using his thumb to wipe it away.

His fingers stayed on my cheek, giving me his hand to lean into for comfort. I could feel his concern for my emotional state. He couldn't comprehend my war of emotions when my head should have been in the clouds.

"I'm scared this means we need to end this," I whispered. "I don't think I am ready for that."

"Oh shit, Princess. We don't have to end this. We don't have to do anything differently." His words were meant to be comforting, but what he didn't realize was that I wanted to do something differently. I wanted to be with him in the open—like my daydream. I couldn't hide him much longer.

"Where do you see this going?"

"Baby, I have been trying to lock you down for a week now. I don't want to lose you either. You have to know how deep this is for me, right?"

I didn't.

Or maybe I did, but I hadn't taken the time to acknowledge it.

Either way, I didn't have a response, so I just kissed him. His hands found the small of my back, and he pulled me in to deepen the kiss. He smelled so good, a mix of freshness from his shower and *him*. That was the first time we had taken any chances at work. Sex against the right-field wall didn't count. We were out of our minds that night.

But that wasn't one of those right field moments. It wasn't a right-field wall, and it was too dangerous for me to risk. So, I gave myself one more taste and backed away.

"Good call, Cupcake. We need to get out of here."

"Yeah, being caught in the janitor's closet with the catcher, five hours after the biggest job offer of my life, isn't a good idea."

"You better go first," he grimaced while adjusting his shorts. "Once again, you are responsible for another one of my boners."

I laughed and elbowed him in his hard stomach before cracking the door slightly open and peeking out. The coast was clear, so I took one last look at Chase, who was now leaning against the opposite wall, watching me with amusement in his eyes. I blew him a kiss and left.

I didn't get any clearer on a decision, but I felt lighter and happier for the first time all day.

That alone spoke to me loud and clear.

chase

Becca and I laid in her bed, satisfied from a fierce round of pent-up sexual energy that almost exploded before we got back to the hotel. When her lips touched mine in that closet, I came close to letting go of any fears of being caught, and fucking her against the door.

It wasn't *my* fears that stopped me. It was her fear. I wouldn't do anything that would risk her future. But I did say a quick thank you to the Gods for her being the one to back away first. Especially when I ran into Kace as I came out of the janitor's closet. Had Becca been seen with me, that shit would have been bad. Instead, he just eyed me like I had lost my mind.

I could handle that.

"What are you thinking about?" she asked as her head rested on my chest, her fingers lightly brushing the patch of hair on my stomach that led below the waistline.

"Nothing." Guys were never thinking about anything, and that was usually a completely honest answer. But then and there, it was a lie, and she called me out on it.

"I can feel you tensing underneath me. Tell me."

Taking a deep breath, I ran a hand through my hair and

considered my words before I spoke. "Just thinking about next week. About how I'm willing to do whatever it takes to make this work. To see this through."

"Really?" She looked up at me, lightness in her eyes.

"Yeah, Baby. Damn. I didn't see this happening, but I don't want us to be over. I also don't want to do anything to make you unhappy. Or make you risk too much. I know how hard you've worked for this." I sighed out of the frustration that I felt at the impossible decision.

"Yeah, I have. But I didn't plan on feeling this way either, Chase."

"I never want to be the reason you have to walk away from your dreams, Becca."

Her eyes glassed over, a mixture of sadness and awe. I wasn't ready to tell her I was falling for her or that I had technically already fallen. But I promised myself that once the dust settled from spring training, and we were still together, I would tell her.

Even though I normally slept like a fucking baby with Becca in my arms, I didn't sleep a wink that night. I had no idea how I was going to play a whole game the next day. The thoughts swirling in my head were a mix of *"I don't want to lose her"* and *"I don't want to hurt her."*

Never in my life had I cared about someone so much—to the point of utter madness. And no matter how many things ran through my head, the one thing I kept coming back to was that I needed to call Tim.

Sitting at my locker, I pressed Tim's name on my phone. He had been in town a couple of days negotiating my new contract, but I needed him to meet with me after the game, even if the negotiations weren't done.

"Just the guy I was about to call," Tim answered.

"Yeah?"

"Contract is ready, Chase. You're going to be a very, very

happy man later today. The Kings don't want to lose you and they're willing to pay top dollar."

"Fuck, that's awesome," I breathed. I had been so wrapped up in Becca, I had forgotten how much I wanted that deal.

"Yeah. So, if that's why you're calling, then worry no more. We're ready to sign when you are."

"Yeah, that's why I was calling." It wasn't, but I suddenly felt guilty for what I had been about to ask of him. He had been working on that deal for me, and I needed to see it through.

As my agent, Tim had just as much to gain from it as I did. That deal would put his name at the top of the industry.

"Okay then, why don't I set the signing for today. Let's get this deal done."

"Yeah, as soon as I am off the field, let's do it."

After letting Tim go, I finished getting dressed and needed to get a wrap on my wrist. That meant I was about to go see Becca. I just wished I could tell her about what was happening, but there would be too many people around.

No one questioned me calling her Princess at work because it started with me trying to drive her crazy. Now, it was just habit. Even when I called her Princess when we were alone, it was just a habit.

So, no one batted an eye when I walked into the training room and said, "Hey Princess."

She spun from where she was writing in a notepad at the high counter along the wall. "Hey Turner, what's up?"

"My wrist." That was all I had to say since I had told her in bed the night before that it was sore. She was the one who told me to wrap it before the game.

Nodding and grabbing some supplies, Becca was in front of me in no time. I hopped onto a table next to Kris, who was getting the same thing done.

"Hey man," Kris jerked his head.

Becca grabbed my arm as I nodded back to Kris, and I had to fight the burn that her touch sent down my body.

"What you got going on tonight?" Kris asked. "I met some girls that might be too much for just me, if you know what I mean."

Raising one eyebrow, I knew exactly what he meant. He wanted me to take one of them off his hands and normally, I would be all about it. Now, I just noticed how Becca stopped moving, how her grip tightened on my arm, and how her eyes tried to stay impassive, but burned in the depths.

"No way. You're on your own," I laughed, trying to play it cool.

"What the hell has gotten into you?" Kris laughed as well, but it was awkward, and he was confused. "You normally have a rotation of women during spring training. These days, you barely show your face."

Becca had started breathing harder, her chest rising rapidly. Kris couldn't see it, but I had explored every inch of her over the last few weeks and I knew her tells.

Shrugging, I hoped to change the subject before Becca got more upset. "Just laying low this year."

"I guess it's working. You're having the best spring of your career, from what I can tell."

"I'm just doing my thing."

"Well, if you want a reward, come out tonight. These girls are just what spring is all about."

I nodded, knowing I wasn't going near another woman. Probably for the rest of my life. No one would ever measure up to what Becca had become to me.

Once Kris finished and left, I looked back to Becca, who had begun wrapping my wrist at an average speed.

"Sorry," I whispered, low enough that the guys across the room couldn't hear.

Her eyes met mine before looking around to see who was

nearby. When she realized no one was too close, she whispered, "He wouldn't have said that if he knew."

She was right. Kris was a good guy. Had he known Becca was my girl, he wouldn't have talked like that to me, especially not in front of her. That was the reason we struggled with hiding our relationship, and it would only get harder as the season went on. Not to mention, the longer I "laid low," the more likely someone would figure me out.

"I'm signing my contract today," I whispered, not wanting to wait to tell her.

Her eyes shot up in the kind of excitement that only someone who truly cared about you could feel. "Oh my God, Chase. I'm so happy for you."

"Want to celebrate tonight?"

"If I had known we would be celebrating, I wouldn't have told my friend that I would have dinner with her tonight."

"Ah, you mentioned she had been texting you."

"Yeah, and I finally caved and said yes."

"How about after?"

"You know I will come straight to you when I'm done."

I smiled, loving her affirmation.

"Unless you're out with Kris," she added, a small smile playing on her lips.

"No way in hell, Princess. I'm yours."

She blushed and finished up the wrap, then her tone turned more professional. "You're all set, Turner."

"Thanks," I said as flatly as possible, jumping down. I took one last look around and then grabbed her hand behind the table where no one could see. I squeezed gently, hoping it translated, and then I walked from the room.

CHAPTER TWENTY-EIGHT

chase

AFTER THE GAME, I WALKED INTO THE BOARDROOM AT THE TOP OF the stadium. That was where I met with the owner, the general manager, Coach, and Tim to lay out the parameters of my new contract offer.

They would give me the details and I would sign. Simple as that.

But as I waited for them to start, my mind drifted again. Back to Becca. The hurt in her eyes at Kris' words. She wasn't jealous, just sad. And I didn't blame her. It was still a daily battle to not hire a banner plane that read "Chase loves Becca" to fly across the city.

"You ready, Chase?" Tim asked.

I nodded and tapped my fingers on the long meeting table we were sitting at. The general manager for the Kings started going down a list of things that would be involved with my contract.

A bonus for so many home runs.

A bonus for so many thrown-out base stealers.

A bonus for a certain number of games played.

The contract was just what I imagined it would be. But I was barely registering with the excitement the way I thought I would. I wasn't humming with the thrill or anxious to sign.

Instead, I found myself interrupting the speech.

"Wait." The room turned silent, and everyone looked at me.

"Any questions, Chase?" Tim asked, concerned about why I was stopping everything.

"Yeah, um…" I trailed off, wondering if what I was about to say was the right thing to do. But I went for it because it felt right. "I want to retire."

The room was silent. No one believed me.

But I meant it.

Baseball was everything to me, until it wasn't. Now Becca was, and her happiness meant more to me than my contract. Was I an idiot to make this decision without talking to her first?

Probably.

Was I stupid for turning down the money and ending my career for a woman I had just met six weeks prior?

Sure.

But I didn't regret the words, and I didn't regret the sentiment. I meant it, and a wave of relief washed over me, knowing that it meant that Becca could have her career, and I could have her—without the lies and secrets from hiding.

"Are you serious?" Tim finally spoke. "You're joking, right?"

I shook my head and sat up in my chair. "I'm not joking. I want to sign retirement papers instead."

The shock on Coach's face was almost funny, and I would have laughed if they wouldn't have thought I was certifiable.

"Chase, you can't be serious. This contract is everything you've wanted," Tim urged.

"I know." I turned to the guys across the table from me. "And I know you all have worked hard for this. But there is something I want more than baseball. And I can't have both. My heart is telling me to hang up my cleats."

"When do you want this to happen?" Coach asked.

"Now?" It was a question because I didn't know how long something like that took to follow through with.

"Chase," the team owner cleared his throat. "That is something we will need to write up and then make an announcement for. We can't make that happen today."

"Tomorrow then?"

"Why don't we give it a few days, see if you still feel the same way. We'll even leave this offer here on the table," he said.

I wouldn't change my mind, but I let him think that was a great idea. At least that would give me time to tell Becca. I could play a few innings and then tell Manny he needed to pray he could pass a drug test because the plate was his.

Standing up, I wanted to get out of there, away from their confused stares. Tim followed me out of the door, ranting and raving about the mistake I was making. He tried to get me to walk back in there and sign. He begged me. He almost fucking cried.

But I stood firm.

I would never regret giving it all up to try and be everything she needed.

With her having dinner with her friend, I had to do my nightly routine alone, which wasn't a big deal since I had it down to an art. So, I was on the floor when a text chimed on my phone.

image sent Same dress. Same result?

I smiled. She was in her sundress. The last time she wore that dress was the first night we were together.

You look beautiful. Definitely the same result.

I feel like I should cancel and come up there with you now. I feel guilty not celebrating with you tonight.

I wanted that, too, but she didn't need to feel guilty, or change her plans. Especially when there was nothing to celebrate. At least not until I told her what happened. And that wasn't something I was forcing.

I'm gonna grab a drink with a few of the guys.

That wasn't the truth, but it would ease her guilt.

Okay, still want me to come up later?

Of course. Text me when you're done at dinner.

xoxo

I laid my phone on the floor beside me, content with not going anywhere. Happy with just waiting for her. I stood up, intending to get a shower, but I didn't make it that far. I was so exhausted, the adrenaline finally causing me to crash. I laid across the bed, intending to give myself a minute. But the next thing I knew, it was eight a.m. and I had slept through the night.

Grabbing my phone, I had several missed calls from Becca, a few texts worried about me, and a final one asking if I had gone out with Kris after all. After everything that happened, I must have been dead to the world.

Running out of my room, I headed to the stadium, while trying to call Becca at the same time. She didn't answer, but since she was supposed to be working, I wasn't shocked. But I was anxious to get to her and let her know everything was okay. Unfortunately, I never got the chance because I walked into a clusterfuck that I was completely unprepared for.

becca

Insecurity was running rampant, and jealousy was rearing its ugly head. I was a mess, going to my own room last night, and I was neurotic when Chase still hadn't answered that morning for PT. A small part of me worried he'd ended up having drinks with Kris, taking him up on the offer to help with his girl situation. What else was I supposed to think?

When it came to Chase, I had a history of overreacting, but something felt off. I felt it before I left to go out with Ali. I could sense it but I just couldn't put my finger on it.

Whatever it was, I came close to canceling dinner with Ali and going straight to Chase. If I didn't need to clear up the fact that I wasn't pregnant, I would have done just that. But Ali and I had barely spoken since I ran from her room feeling sick. I needed to show her I was okay and make her believe that I wasn't pregnant.

"Becca, come in here, please," Gary shouted as I passed his open office door.

"Sir?" I asked, popping my head in.

"We're ready to sign you on. You ready?"

I wasn't.

In fact, after the day I had, I knew I never would be.

It wasn't just that I wanted to be with Chase. It was that even if we broke it off, I would never be able to work that closely with him and not want to tear his eyes out every time Kris suggested they go out. Or tear his close off every time he called me Cupcake.

The second I fell for Chase was the second I lost the job for good.

"Gary. I can't take the job."

"Excuse me?" Gary's eyes almost fell out of his head.

I tried to smile to lighten the mood, but he needed to know so he could offer the job to one of the other guys.

"I'm so sorry. This has been the best experience of my career. I came here wanting nothing more than to work for this team. But…" I paced a little, eager to get done and find Chase, but also reluctant to finish my sentence. "Things have changed over the last few weeks, and now I think I need to take a step back and think about what I need to do."

"What could have changed? I don't understand. Are the players giving you shit? Is this anything we can fix?"

"I am thankful for this opportunity." I continued as a tear fell down my cheek. I didn't plan on having that conversation first thing in the morning. I didn't even realize that was my plan until it came out of my mouth. "I'm going to finish the spring out. I know you need all the hands you can get for the next few days."

"We can offer you more, Becca. I really don't want to lose your experience and aptitude. You've been just what we needed here. What can I do to change your mind?"

"Nothing." Another tear escaped, so I mumbled something about needing to work and ran from the office.

I felt dizzy. The morning was already too much. My head was pounding. My arms were shaking.

I wanted Chase.

I needed Chase.

Where the hell was he?

Then, it finally happened. Five minutes later, when I walked into the locker room, my head finally exploded.

becca

"What the fuck, Chase? What the hell do you think you're doing?"

That was the first thing I heard when I walked into the locker room and I stopped just inside the doorway as Ethan charged from his locker to Chase's.

"What *am* I doing?" Chase asked, pulling a shirt over his head and running his arms through it.

"I just talked to Tim. You wanna tell me what in the actual fuck you're thinking?"

"What business is it of yours? Just because we share an agent doesn't mean we share all our secrets. What made Tim think he had a right to tell you anything?"

"He wants me to talk you out of being stupid. Apparently, I have two hours to accomplish that before you sign your life away."

"What's going on?" Kace asked.

"Yeah, what the hell are you two fighting about?" Fernandez stood from his stool near Chase's.

Kris and a few other guys walked in to see what was happening. Keith and Eddie also stopped their conversation to watch. It was still early, so the locker room wasn't full, but there was an audience, nonetheless. No one seemed to notice that I was standing by the door, frozen in place, wondering what Ethan was so upset about.

"Nothing!" Chase yelled, answering everyone that was watching.

"It's *not* nothing," Ethan yelled. "Chase refused his big ass contract yesterday, and made a motion to retire."

Retire? I must have gasped louder than I thought because all heads turned toward me, finally realizing I was there.

"Oh my God, no," I whispered, shaking my head and putting my hands over my mouth.

Chase was eyeing me, gauging my reaction without being obvious that my reaction was the one he cared about. He had a bag in his hand, and his locker looked emptier as if he had been cleaning it out.

Oh God. He's for real.

"What do you care?" Chase finally turned away from me and asked Ethan.

"You're my catcher. You're my partner. And you just up and decide to leave me and the team three days before the season starts? It's fucked up, Turner."

"I didn't make this decision to hurt your little feelings, Jones. I made it for me. There's something else I need to see through right now. It's personal."

Ethan started to get upset again, but Kace spoke up before any words left his mouth.

"He's right, Ethan. He has some things he needs to work through."

Chase looked at him, questioning in his eyes.

Then he looked at me, silently asking how much Kace knew about us. I shook my head as slightly as I could, my eyes still wide and my hands still on my face.

"What do you know about what I'm going through?" Chase

asked, daring Kace to speak up. Kace wouldn't hurt me in front of everyone, and Chase took that chance by calling him out. But Kace looked to Kris, who nodded at him to keep going.

"We know you're struggling with alcohol, man. I think you need to get right. It's more important than the game right now."

Now, my head was really spinning. What was happening? Chase had alcohol issues? Chase never drank when we were together. And I never tasted it on his lips.

"What in the hell are you talking about?" Chase asked, sincerely looking confused.

"You're car. It's fucked up. You're not hanging out anymore. The one night you did hang out you downed a ton of whiskey in record time and then bailed on us. We rode to the bar in your car. Cam saw AA and rehab pamphlets shoved under the seat. The receipts for all the liquor stuffed in the backseat."

Chase had his head down, his hands on his hips. He was shaking his head in denial, but not saying anything. Once his head popped up, he sighed in resignation. "No sense in lying anymore."

"So, you do have a problem?" Fernandez asked, almost giddy over the idea of Chase having a major flaw.

"No. I don't," Chase stated, "But my dad does. The receipts were his. The pamphlets were things I picked up randomly, hoping I could find one for him."

The guys, including myself, took a step back. No one was going to condemn Chase for anything his dad did. But why keep it a secret? Why hide it? Why lie?

Suddenly, I didn't feel like I knew Chase as well as I thought. We had shared so much, but not once did he feel comfortable enough to confide in me about the struggles with his dad.

I was a hypocrite.

"I don't buy that shit. Or maybe you and daddy both have a taste for the hard stuff," Fernandez poked.

Chase rolled his eyes and scoffed, "That's rich, coming from someone who takes *'vitamins'* every morning. You may want to double-check that label because, after today, you're gonna get more piss tests than Lance Armstrong."

"What the fuck are you talking about?" Fernandez yelled and looked my way. I was the one who had caught him taking the pills, and he knew I was the one who had said something.

"Don't look at her," Chase yelled. "This has nothing to do with her. All I'm saying is that you need to worry about yourself."

"Wait," Kace stepped up, "Fernandez? What the fuck?"

"Don't even, Cap. Turner over here is taking the word of an intern. An intern that Keith has been fucking behind the scenes for a while now." Then he looked at me again. "You can't throw stones when you are over there sinning yourself, Babydoll."

What in the actual fuck? Did he just say I was sleeping with Keith? How in the hell did we get that far? I started breathing hard, shaking my head 'no' again in denial. I eyed everyone, all eyes back on me.

Did they believe that? I looked at Keith, who looked ready to throw up. But he wasn't denying anything.

"I heard Keith on the phone, Turner. I handed that information to you and told you to get his head back in the game. Instead, you do what? Ignore me."

"You had it out for Becca," Chase yelled. "I had no reason to believe you."

"You believe me now? Because Keith over there isn't exactly denying it, are you, lover boy?" Fernandez was wrong. I had never even spoken more than four words to Keith.

I was mortified and I couldn't speak. I just kept shaking my head and looking toward Keith, begging him to speak for me. Begging him to tell the truth. What did he have to gain from lying?

But he never opened his mouth.

He took two steps back, apologizing to me with his pained expression but never admitting the truth. Chase eyed us back and forth, debating on what he was going to believe. It was the first time I had seen questions in his eyes directed at me, which hurt.

Kace was also looking at me, disbelieving.

Then, like a bolt of lightning, it hit me. From somewhere deep inside, I knew the truth. And as much as I didn't want to hurt Keith, I had to stop the lies once and for all.

My throat was dry. My head hurt. I felt sick to my stomach. But I somehow managed the one word I needed to.

"Jason."

becca

Everyone turned from me back to Keith. He still wasn't saying anything, but he didn't have to. The truth was in his eyes.

The fear of being outed.

The fear of being exiled.

Judged.

Labeled.

Condemned

He wouldn't feel that from me. Chase either. And I knew Kace wouldn't judge either. But not everyone was tolerant and accepting of the differences we all faced. So, I understood Keith's desire for privacy and peace.

Unfortunately, I wasn't going to be his excuse. That wasn't fair to me, or Chase. That was his lie, and I had enough of my own to be concerned with. I didn't care if everyone knew I was with Chase, but Chase needed to realize I hadn't been with Keith.

"Jason?" Kace asked.

"The other intern?" Chase questioned.

Keith didn't deny or confirm. He just lowered his head even more.

"Is that why he got fired?" Ethan wondered.

Of course, it was. Gary didn't tell a soul why Jason was let go, but he wouldn't. It wasn't his place. Keeping that matter private was all Gary cared about.

But the pieces fit.

We just had to keep Fernandez from being a dick about it, because I knew he would be the first one to talk shit.

"This was last week. Jason is long gone," Fernandez tried to reason.

By some grace and divine intervention, Keith finally spoke up. "He's still in town. Still here." He cleared his throat before continuing, "For me." He shrugged and looked pained, but he spoke, and that was all that mattered.

He looked like he could use a hug, but he saluted everyone and walked backward, deciding he had heard enough and was no longer curious how everything would play out.

Lucky.

I wanted to follow him. I no longer cared how it all turned out, either. But I was still frozen in place, standing by the door feeling physically ill at everything being laid out among the guys. Chase and I had a lot to discuss, but it wasn't the time. He needed to make things right with the guys first—his team, his family.

Yet, I didn't move.

It was like riding past an accident where you couldn't help but look.

You'd think that would have been enough, that everyone would stand down. But Fernandez was still there, and he was out for blood.

"Whatever," Manny looked my way. "I still think you and Keith have been going at it. I've been watching you; you're definitely getting some." He made noise and shook his head.

He made me so damn angry. I was tired of hiding how I felt about Chase. I was tired of the idea that he and I being together was wrong. I had already turned my job down. I had already decided to give in, so why wait any longer? My need to defend Chase and me was deeper than my need to save face.

But I had been a liar. I hadn't told him my truth any more than he had told me his. Sure, maybe we could talk things out. Maybe we could survive.

Maybe not.

In that moment, all I knew was he couldn't make a retirement decision without it all being on the table. Unfortunately, we didn't have that kind of time.

"I have been, Manny, you're right," I confessed. All eyes turned to me and my bravado waivered a little, making my breathing more labored. My vision was blurry and my head was still pounding. But I couldn't do it anymore.

I was done.

When I looked up at Chase, I made it clear who I was with even without saying the words. I loved him and I hoped he forgave me for what I was about to do. Because, above all else, he needed to know everything.

"You can't retire," I whispered.

"We can talk about it later," he tried shutting me down.

"I don't see the point; I can't lie anymore, Chase." And I didn't just mean about us. I couldn't lie about *me*, either.

I wouldn't let him end his career for me when he didn't know who I was and what a future with me entailed. It was time to stop distracting him and avoiding it all. He needed to know before he signed on the dotted line. He was nearing the end of his career and I knew he would resent me when all my lies came tumbling out.

"I'm done. I turned down the job. I'm leaving. I failed. And now I need space."

My words were broken through my inability to get a deep breath. I just hoped it made sense.

I was outing us.
I was protecting us.
I was defending us.
I was ending us.

chase

WHAT WAS SHE DOING?

She didn't want everyone to think she was with Keith, so I understood her need to out us, but she was done? I didn't fucking think so.

I was willing to give up everything for her. She owed me more than just ending things without even giving us a chance to talk. It didn't matter that I was supposed to sign my retirement papers soon, she wasn't going to force my hand.

"What are you saying, Princess?" It was obvious, and with all eyes on us, I shouldn't have even asked, but she started it and I could barely move my feet.

"You will resent me. You will change your mind." Tears streamed down her face, and her body was shaking, making me want to scoop her into my arms.

"I won't." I took a few steps toward her, I stopped when she took those same steps backward, not wanting me to get closer.

"You don't even know me," she cried.

"I know what I need to know, Baby."

Right then, the other guys caught on, and I heard their responses behind me.

"Holy shit," Ethan muttered.

"I knew she was getting some," Fernandez shouted. "This explains so fucking much, though. Should have known it was Turner's dick she was riding."

The need to punch his face in again was the only thing distracting me from Becca and I started his way, set on drawing blood. But I was pulled back, turned around, and in my face was Kace, realizing that Becca and I had been lying to him.

His face was red. His eyes were so sharp he could have cut me open. He was breathing so hard I thought he was going to pass out. I knew he would be pissed, but his rage was next level. I wanted to tell him to back off, that he wasn't Becca's keeper, that she was a big girl.

But he beat me to the battle, and his words ended the war.

"You knocked up Cam's sister?"

The entire locker room gasped and then went silent.

Did I just hear him correctly? Surely, I was in some fucking dream, and I would wake up any second. My stare turned back to Becca, whose eyes were bigger than they had been since the entire clusterfuck started. She had a hand over her stomach, her head was bouncing around not confirming yes or no, and her skin was pale. But Kace had given me new eyes with just nine words, and when I looked at her through those eyes... I saw it.

Cam.

Her familiarity.

Her vague answers about her brother.

Her avoiding telling me her last name.

Kace's connection to her.

She knew I was friends with Cam. I had even talked about him, and gone out with him. I would come back and tell her about "*my friend Cam*," and she never said a word. My shock was enough to make Kace back off, and he dropped my bunched-up shirt he had grabbed and ran a hand down his face.

"You didn't know," he whispered, connecting the dots between my shock and Becca's panic.

I wasn't even giving that statement the satisfaction of a response because, no, the fuck, I didn't know.

But Becca had been right after all. I didn't know her. She didn't give me the chance to know her. I was ending my career for someone I didn't know all because I fell in love with who I thought she was.

Being Cam's sister wasn't a deal-breaker. She could have told me, and we would have been fine. The problem was the lie. And after having chance after chance, she never chose to tell me the truth.

Disconcerted and angry, I had nothing to say. Fernandez was laughing. Ethan was saying, "*Fuck*," over and over again. Kris and most of the others had decided to leave. Kace was looking between me and Becca.

Becca was wobbling, disoriented, and sweating.

And then it clicked—Kace's entire statement—and I turned as white as a ghost.

"You're pregnant?"

Instead of answering, she fell, succumbing to the insanity and madness. Her body gave in to the shock as she fainted and landed hard on her shoulder.

Kace and I, along with Ethan, rushed to her, and instead of being angry, I was panicking. Fear of her being hurt took over every feeling I had before that. But I couldn't get to her as Kace pushed me away with all his force.

"If you were willing to disappear after getting her pregnant, then you don't need to be here for her now."

That gave me a whole new set of questions and concerns. How in the hell could he think I would leave her after knocking her up? Fuck, I didn't even know I had knocked her up. She told me she was on birth control.

The day was out of control, and it was still morning. And somehow, we all still had to play a game in a few hours.

Kace picked up Becca, who had come to and was moaning that her arms hurt. I was close behind, worried about her and...a baby?

Our baby?

Holy fuck.

No way.

A baby?

I stopped in the hallway, catching my breath as Kace continued toward Gary's office. Leaning against the cold wall as my teammates passed me on their way in for the day, they all asked if I was okay, oblivious to the shitshow they had just missed. I nodded, but I never spoke, concentrating on my breathing, and trying not to faint the way Becca had.

We needed to talk and make decisions and it felt urgent. Yet, I couldn't bring myself to go to her. Not until I was put back together and settled some other things.

becca

I was back in my room, curled into a ball and holding a pillow to my chest. The tears had started right after I realized I was in Gary's office, on his couch.

Again.

He was hovering over me, asking me to blink once, to follow his fingers, and anything else he thought would verify I was okay. I must have passed his test because he let Kace take me back to my room with a few ibuprofen for the pain in my arm.

I didn't even ask or wonder if Gary knew what had happened. Word was going to travel fast through the locker room and he would be filled in. Then he would understand why I turned the job down.

Kace got me back to my room, where Cam and Ali were waiting when we arrived. Like a TV playing in the background, I listened as Kace told Cam and Ali everything that had happened. It felt like they were far away, but they were standing right next to me as Ali was gently rubbing my back while I nestled into the pillow.

I knew how the story went. I remembered everything up until I passed out. And the truth of that was hard to listen to.

"Chase just bailed. I snapped at him, but I thought he was behind us. He never showed back up." Kace explained.

"I'm going to kill him," Cam seethed, pacing the room at the foot of the bed.

"She never told him she was your sister."

"It doesn't fucking matter. She needs him. I don't care who she is, he needs to grow the fuck up."

There were so many lies still swirling around and I needed to interject. I needed to speak up. But when I opened my mouth, only a hoarse croaking noise came out, urging Ali to shush me and rub my back more.

The explosion of lies had been more than I could handle. But the look in Chase's eyes when he learned I was Cam's sister was gut-wrenching.

I was going to tell him. I had to. But I couldn't let him retire before I had that chance. Ending us was the only sure way to change his mind before it was too late. Ethan had said as much. Chase had to 'sign his life away' in a few hours.

Sleep took over for a while, and I stirred away when I heard the door clicking shut.

"Who left?" with my voice barely above a whisper.

"Cam went to grab me some things from our room, so I can stay here with you tonight," Ali responded from behind me on the bed.

Realizing the light had faded, I shot upright, feeling better than I had earlier.

"What time is it?"

"It's only six."

"I need to call Chase," I moaned, reaching for my phone.

"No one has heard from him since you passed out in the locker room. Kace went back to the stadium to play today, and he told me Chase never showed up for the game either. He needs to get his shit together."

"Ali, this was all just as big of a shock to him as it was to me.

He found out in the bluntest way possible that I had lied to him. And right after he told everyone he was retiring—for me. He's probably embarrassed and pissed. I know I am."

"Sure, sure. But you already told me the guy you were seeing bailed on you, Ali. Now we know that guy is Chase. And to top it off, he ran away again, right after finding out you were pregnant."

Oh shit. I had almost forgotten that part.

"I'm not pregnant," I said sternly. "He didn't bail on me. I lied. I didn't want Cam and Kace to know, so I lied to you, I lied to them. It was Chase all along, and he never bailed. Instead, I lied to him too, so scared if he knew I was Cam's sister that whatever we had would be over. I told you last night I wasn't pregnant."

Fresh tears started streaming down my face. Chase would never forgive me for the mess I had created. Ali, Cam, and Kace may never forgive me either. I should have been honest with everyone from the beginning. But after the first lie, the second lie was instinct.

The third lie was self-preservation.

The fourth lie was selfishness.

The fifth lie was for Chase.

They all just tumbled out, and I no longer knew who knew what anymore.

"You never told him who you were?" Ali asked hesitant as she too was piecing everything together.

"It would have changed things. At least I was scared it would. I just needed more time."

"And you're not pregnant?" She confirmed again.

"No," I mumbled. "I've just been so damn stressed."

Ali sighed again, clearly annoyed, but somehow feeling like she needed to apologize. "Sorry I got the guys so worked up thinking you were pregnant, Becs. It just all kind of made sense, and you left without a word when you escaped to the bathroom. I know you told me you weren't pregnant at dinner, but you weren't very convincing."

I finally laughed, the situation being too absurd to not find it just a bit funny. Or maybe I was hysterical. But after my giggles subsided, I laid back on the bed and looked at the ceiling, one thing going through my mind.

"I need him, Ali."

"I know, Becs. Just remember, though. No matter how this all ends up, he still believes you're pregnant, and he's nowhere to be found."

chase

I HAD LEFT THE STADIUM, INTENT ON TAKING CARE OF TWO THINGS before talking to Becca—my contract and my dad.

It took all day, but I made it back to the stadium, needing just a few more minutes to collect my thoughts and return some things to my locker. It was empty and dark, just the emergency lights glowing in certain spaces. Like the corner where Becca and I had all our dinners before physical therapy. Where we learned about one another with our conversations. And probably where I was the first time I knew I was in love with her.

Strolling through the training room, I looked around and touched the surfaces as I passed, wondering why I had gone back there first. But it was her space—our space—and I wanted a quick reminder of our spring together.

After leaving the training room, I headed into the locker room and sat in front of my locker. I unpacked the small bag I had packed earlier that morning when I was there.

My cleats back in their place.

My favorite mitt back in its place.

My shower sandals.

My deodorant.

A pic of my mom.

All put back in their place.

Instead of heading out, I walked through the double doors that led to the field. The tunnel was dark and seemed longer than it really was, but I could see the light at the end, calling me toward it.

Though the dugout, I walked up the steps and onto the field then took a deep breath of the fresh air, taking in the lights, the seats, and home plate. The stadium wasn't as big as our stadium back in Atlanta, but it was what the game was all about. Spring training was everything to a ballplayer. From the time we got our first hit in Little League, that was where we dreamt of being.

Walking out a little farther, I stopped when I realized I wasn't alone. Off in the distance, near the right-field wall, I saw her.

Becca.

She was sitting down, back against the wall, knees up, and her head was down. From what I could tell, she hadn't realized I was there. And had I not known her so well, I wouldn't have been able to tell if it was even her with the darkness and distance making it hard to see.

I started walking slowly toward her, wanting to get as far as possible before she noticed I was there because I was kind of scared she would run. Scared, she wouldn't want to talk about anything yet. But if I could get close enough, I knew I had a chance.

Once I was about twenty feet away, she must have sensed my approach and looked up, eyes wide and tears streaking her face. My steps got faster, instinct telling me to get to her, to save her from whatever she was feeling and thinking. And much to my shock, she didn't try running or keeping me from approaching. She just waited and watched as I slid my hands in my pockets and looked down at her.

"What are you doing out here?"

"Ali was smothering me," she shrugged. "So I went for a walk and ended up here."

Ali. Her friend. The one she's been hanging out with on occasion. Cam and Kace's girl.

How had I never made that connection? Obviously, if she was friends with Kace, then she was friends with Ali. That much I should have known.

Not wanting to mention how much it stung, I nodded and laughed a little, making her eyes get big with questioning.

"Isla," I said simply, answering her unspoken question. "The night I went out with Cam and Kace, Ali was saying goodbye to them, saying she had to go slay Isla or something like that. I just now realized how that all connects. You told her about Isla."

"Yeah," she smiled sheepishly. "I was having a hard time keeping my feelings a secret."

"You did better than you thought." I didn't mean it as harshly as it sounded. But her eyes glassed over, and she turned her head away. With the right field wall behind her, it was the perfect place to talk, so I got closer and sat beside her.

"Cam's your brother?" It was obvious, but I asked anyway.

"Yep."

"Wanna tell me the whole story?"

"I might as well," she breathed, looking my way.

And then she started. From her expectations of being related to football royalty, to the drive to do something without Cam's attachment, to getting the job with the Kings. She told me how she begged Kace to act like he didn't know her. How she panicked that he had told me. How she lied to Ali when she realized she had given too much away and was scared she might tell Kace and Cam.

I took it all in, quietly absorbing the sting and blows as I learned her little truths. I was angry, but I had to acknowledge that I hadn't been completely honest with her either.

So after she spoke, I told her about my dad. About the

offseason I spent babysitting him. How he drove my car down to Florida and dented it up. I told her that was where I had been the night I didn't show up for my physical, and how I didn't want the team to know I had an underlying distraction off the field.

"Your lies weren't as bad as mine," she sighed when I was all done.

"Lies are lies, Princess."

"Cam is your friend though. I should have told you the second we decided to be together."

"Eh, Cam only comes around for Kace, it's not like we get our nails done and drink mimosas on Sundays together."

She smiled and it felt good seeing her smile again. Her smile made me smile.

"What now?"

"Now," I sighed, my smile falling. "Now we get to the hard stuff."

becca

ALI HAD BEEN DRIVING ME CRAZY. IF SHE WASN'T TENDING TO MY every need, she was telling me how awful Chase was for disappearing.

I had to get out of there so I told her I was walking to the ice machine, but I was four blocks away before I decided to text her and tell her I wasn't coming back for a while, and needed air.

Ending up at the stadium, I headed straight to the right-field wall, trying to find some peace in the chaos of my brain. Everything in me wanted to call Chase but I refrained, knowing Kace had already tried. I was afraid he would ignore my call as well, and I wasn't ready to find out if that was the case.

It shouldn't have been surprising that Chase showed up to the field. It was like we were drawn to each other, whether we liked it or not. And when he sat down next to me, the weight I had been carrying on my chest eased up.

I told him everything. My entire story, making sure he knew that my lies were never intended to hurt him. It was all about protecting myself, and I hoped he understood. Even if we couldn't move past it, we were at least getting closure.

"You're not pregnant, are you?" he asked, but also sounding certain.

"No, but Ali thought I was when I got sick. I was an idiot, and instead of denying it, I ran away, not wanting to risk telling her about you. Of course she told Kace and Cam. Which bothered me at first, but now that I see how messed up it makes everything, I'm glad she didn't lie for me. The lies have made me sick and stressed. The closer we got, the more I knew I needed to confess, but I got so scared."

"You took a test or something? You could have told me if you did." He reached for my hand and squeezed. "I would have been there for you. You could have been honest and not been alone."

"Where have you been all day, then?" I bit at him, instantly regretting it.

He blanched at my sudden snap, and withdrew his hand from mine. "Seeing Kace carrying you to Gary's office, so pissed at me for my ignorance, like I just knocked you up and left you in the lurch, it was a lot. I had no idea what he was getting at, or what he meant, so I backed off, needing to think. To make sure I wasn't missing something I should have seen."

"But why disappear for so long?"

"Well, first of all, I realized you weren't pregnant. We may have had a lot of lies between us, but in my gut, I felt you would have told me if your test was positive. I trusted you in that moment. It wasn't the kind of thing I felt you would have misled me about."

"I did lie, though. I'm not on birth control."

"You're not pregnant either, though, are you?" He repeated his earlier question.

"No. I can't have kids," I confessed and started crying again. "My mom and dad are the only other people that know. I got sick and had an infection when I was a teenager. Whatever. The point is, I wanted you to trust me, but I didn't want to tell you the truth. I was afraid it would scare you away because some of your random questions had been about kids."

"Princess," he whispered. "That wouldn't have changed how I feel about you. You know that, right?"

I shrugged. Unsure. "Ali doesn't even know. I didn't even tell her when she thought I was pregnant, but I should have. All this embarrassment could have been avoided. Maybe even all this heartache, because all this has done is remind me of something I can never have."

Chase took a deep breath and grabbed my hand again. He brought it to his lips and kissed my fingers, willing my sadness away.

"I know that it is something we could have talked about. And we would have, eventually. I was going to tell you everything."

"But then this morning happened?"

"Yeah."

"Fucking Ethan," Chase laughed.

"Fucking Chase," I corrected him. He looked at me, confused. "What were you thinking? Retiring?"

"I wanted you to have your dream job, and I wanted to have you. It wasn't that hard of a decision once I realized it."

"I could never let you leave this game for me. I would feel too much pressure. I mean, look at us, we are a couple of liars. We shouldn't be making major life decisions."

He laughed again, that time with humor vibrating his chest, making me swat at him playfully.

"You turned your job down, didn't you?" he asked when he finally stopped laughing.

"Yeah."

"So, you made a major life decision, too. For me."

"Yeah, I guess I'm just as dumb as you are."

"We are a match made in heaven."

We sat there in silence for a while. The heaviness of the day was beginning to subside and I was feeling better. When I told Ali

I needed him, that moment was what I meant. Whether we were together in a relationship, friends, or coworkers. I knew we would never be enemies.

I needed him.

"What now, Chase?"

He shrugged but pulled my hand, lifting me and grabbing my waist to straddle him. "I don't know, Cupcake. We have a lot to talk about."

I nodded, my forehead falling to his. I thought maybe he and I were done. That we couldn't make it through all the lies we told. But maybe we could.

"We have a lot to learn about one another," he continued, and I just kept nodding in agreement. "I don't really know what is going to happen."

A small tear escaped my eye at his truthful words. I didn't know either.

He took his thumb and wiped away my tear then kissed my cheek.

"The only thing I know for sure," he continued. "Is that I am going to have so much fun pissing Cam off when I tell him how much I love his sister."

I barked an unexpected laugh, but sobered up when it hit me.

"You love me?"

"Don't act like you didn't know."

I didn't know.

I had hoped. I had wished.

"Are you sure you're not lying?" I asked with a smirk on my face.

"No more lies."

"No more lies," I repeated. "And I love you too."

CHAPTER THIRTY-SIX

chase

BECCA AND I STAYED IN EACH OTHER'S ARMS AGAINST THE RIGHT field wall for a little longer.

She was crazy if she thought I would let her go. That was never an option.

Was I confused by the truths?

Yes.

Was I hurt by the lies?

Oh yeah.

Did that change how I felt about her?

Not even a little bit.

Pregnant, not pregnant, Cam's sister, whatever. As long as she wasn't *my* sister, I was all in with her. And she loved me. I knew she did. That was why when I left the stadium earlier, my decisions were easy, just time-consuming.

"Second of all?" she asked abruptly.

I pulled back and looked at her, confused. We had been quiet for so long, I had almost forgotten that I left some more details lingering.

"You said earlier, *'first of all'*... But you never told me what second of all was."

"Yeah," I nodded. "Second of all. I had to make arrangements regarding my contract with the team. It took longer than I expected."

Now she was nodding, acknowledging she knew I needed to take care of that. But I could tell that whatever she was thinking was wrong.

"I'm going to play the rest of spring training, that's why I ended up here tonight. To bring my things back for the three days we have left."

"I expected that. I'm so relieved."

"Then I am done, Princess."

She pulled back to look me in my eyes, concern in her features.

"There were two things I had to do when I left the stadium," I reexplained. "Finish signing my retirement papers, and arrange rehab for my dad. Both took time, but they're done."

"Chase, no."

"Shhh," I calmed her down by stroking her bottom lip. "I didn't make that decision for you, I made it for me. I need to stop hiding from my dad and help him. When he lost my mom, he started drinking. I was all he had, and I just ignored him. Shit, I lost you for an afternoon and I was tempted to drink. I cannot image how he must feel every day."

There was no comparison to my dad's loss. I couldn't even fathom that kind of loss. But it made me realize I needed to be there for him. I called him and we had a long talk. I told him my plans, and he agreed to try rehab.

But there were more reasons for my decision.

"I also need to stop putting a band-aid on these old knees, and start being more careful. I am only thirty-three years old. Whether you were pregnant or not, it made me consider that eventually, I might have a reason to want to walk without pain."

The constant flow of tears that Becca seemed to have, started their tracks down her cheek again. Her bottom lip trembled.

"I have more money than I will ever need. I have already proven I'm one of the best catchers to ever play the game. I've had an amazing career. I'm okay with being done. I'm ready. And yeah, falling in love with you may have played a role in my decision, but it wasn't just you. It was the perspective that those feelings gave me."

"I hope you know that even by retiring, I still don't think I can take that job. After the scene that played out in there, I'm not even sure I can show my face to finish spring training."

"I'll support whatever you do, Princess. But I can promise you one thing, no one is going to even look at you funny with Kace and me breathing down their necks."

"Kace is mad at you," she reminded me.

"Yeah but he's not mad at you. Plus, he'll get over it."

She smiled and leaned in to kiss me. It was our first kiss again. The one where we let everything else go and chose to be together despite whatever was ahead. And just like the first kiss, it was not going to be enough.

Gripping her ass, I lifted her in the air as I stood and started walking off the field with her.

"Where're we going?" she asked, trying to look back at the direction we were headed.

"The bullpen. Wanna make sure the right field wall isn't the only place we cover out here."

That gorgeous laugh bloomed out of her again and warmed everything inside me. I was going to spend the rest of my life making her laugh and keeping those tracks of tears away.

"What happens if someone asks if we had sex in the bullpen?"

I pulled back but kept my stride. "Why would anyone ask that?"

She shrugged. "Just want to be prepared."

I smiled and shook my head at her. "Then we lie, Cupcake."

CHAPTER THIRTY-SEVEN

becca

It was the bottom of the ninth, with two runners on base, and the Kings were down by two runs. Chase was on deck, and since they were intentionally walking Kace in front of him, he was about to get a chance at one last at-bat with the bases loaded.

Three days had passed since the bomb went off in the locker room, and now Chase was playing his very last game. True to my word, I worked the last few days of spring training, and Chase was right, no one even looked at me the wrong way. But after coming clean to Gary, he agreed to let me be a fan for Chase's last game, so I sat in the stands with Ali and Cam to my right, and the owner of the Kings to my left.

It was strange how accepting everyone was despite all the rules I broke. Chase had told me to tell Gary everything, so I did. Even the part where I lied about Manny, and falling in love with Chase. When I told him who my brother was, he sputtered and spit, then told me it was all okay.

It wasn't. I had more red flags than the beach during a hurricane. But I took pride in the fact that he offered me the job before he knew about Cam's influence.

In good conscience, I still turned down his offer for the job.

But he had insisted it had nothing to do with Cam, and was making me temped to accept.

"Pssst." Looking up, I saw Chase smiling at me from on the deck circle. "Eyes up here, Princess."

Turning red, I looked away quickly, not wanting anyone else to see me blushing. Ali was giggling, though, and Cam was making a gagging noise like he was twelve. Ali, Cam, and Kace were waiting for me when I returned to my room. Chase was with me and we all sat down and talked about everything that has transpired all spring. We even laughed as I told them about texting Ali while she talked to Kace on that first day, and how I called Chase 'Butter Boy.'

Once everyone realized Chase didn't leave me knocked up, when they knew for sure that we were okay, and it was going to be okay between us, everything fell into place. Cam threatened Chase a few times, but Chase had said he expected nothing less. He also vowed to take care of me, waggling his eyebrows and making Cam gag. It made me fall even more in love with him.

The days that followed were spent relearning everything about one another. We retold stories and shared new ones, things I had never told anyone.

Chase and I felt free. And with freedom came truths.

"Now batting for the Kings, Chase Turner." The PA announcer caught my attention when I heard his voice.

Chase had announced his retirement a few days before, so the crowd roared, knowing that it was the last at-bat of Chase's career.

He walked to the plate and tipped his hat to the fans, thanking them for their love. He hit the bat on his shoes several times and settled into his stance, waiting on the pitch. After a few balls and a strike, he finally got the pitch he wanted and swung.

The ball flew towards the right-field wall, and with two outs, the runners had taken off, rounding the bases quicker than the ball could even land. The right fielder jumped but missed, and like something written in a novel, the ball ricocheted off the exact spot that Chase and I now considered "our spot."

The fans screamed as Kace crossed home plate with the winning run. The players piled on Chase like it was game seven of the World Series. It was a moment he deserved, and I was honored to watch and cheer him on.

When everyone settled down, he was pulled to the side by the media for an interview. Kace had come to get me to join them on the field and I stood behind the camera so I couldn't be seen but was close enough to hear.

"Chase, what was going through your mind, knowing this was your last at-bat in a Kings' uniform?"

"I just wanted to give my teammates a high before the season starts. I want them going in with a win, and knowing they got this from here on out."

"Will we see you around the stadium this season, in a supporting role?"

"Maybe. If the guys need me for a pep talk, I'll be there."

"Now that you have ended your career in epic fashion, what are you going to do next?"

"I'm going to Disney World!"

Chase

I thought retirement would be harder than it was, but the adjustment was welcoming in a way I couldn't have imagined. Not only did I get to spend time with Becca whenever I wanted, but I reconnected with my dad as well.

After a month in rehab, we sold the house he shared with my mom and he got his own place near Atlanta. He had to move forward and going back to his old house would have been a trigger for him. Since he wasn't drinking, I loved being around him more.

Becca ended up taking a deal with the Kings that allowed her to work with the team as needed. It gave her a little taste of being with a pro team, but I could tell she was gravitating back toward the high school kids. She even asked me to volunteer at the school, and I could picture myself being a coach somewhere down the line.

Not until after I finished my to-do list, though. For starters, I created a charity golf tournament to raise money for kids in the Atlanta area that needed safer sports equipment. As a catcher, I knew how important it was to stay safe, and a lot of kids couldn't afford the proper helmets and chest guards, especially year after year as they grew.

One day, with Becca's help, I wanted to expand the initiative to the entire state, and maybe even surrounding areas. Giving back became my new purpose, and it was more fulfilling than playing ever was.

Also on my to-do list was to get Becca to move in with me. She tried to tell me it was too soon and she wasn't sure it was a good idea. But two months went by and we never spent a night alone. Either at her place or mine, we were together, and she eventually realized making two rent payments was ridiculous.

The final thing on my post-retirement to-do list was to get Becca to marry me. I had never made it a secret that I planned on being with her forever, and I was finally going to make it official.

I had already spoken to her father, and Cam. I even ran it past Kace and Ali, wanting their approval as well. Not that it would have made a difference. The Pope could have told me no and I would still have thrown myself at Becca's feet and begged her to be mine forever.

KACE

Becca just left the stadium. Good luck tonight.

I'm shaking like a rookie.

We were back in Florida for spring training again, only I wasn't a player and Becca wasn't an intern. She had been asked to be the assistant trainer for Gary while his primary guy took paternity time off. For me, I just followed her down there and spent a lot of time sneaking her to the bullpen and the right field wall.

After ten minutes, I went down to the lobby and met her as she got off the shuttle. She had already changed and knew I wanted to take her out, so she was as ready as she needed to be.

"How was work?" I asked casually, trying to sound normal.

"Good! What did you get into today?"

"Nothing," I lied. It was okay, though. That lie was for the sake of her surprise and she would forgive me once she saw how I really spent my day.

"Nothing?" She laughed, already not believing me. "You're always into something."

"Saved my energy for tonight," I waggled my eyebrows at her, making her laugh, and led her to the valet to get my car.

Once we were settled in, I started driving in a familiar direction, but I hoped that running my hands up her bare thighs and under her skirt was enough of a distraction. She moaned as my fingers grazed the outside of her thin panties and I could feel the heat starting to saturate the fabric.

"Fuck Cupcake. Don't make me pull the car over."

"You started it," she moaned, moving her hips so that she could get more friction from my fingers.

My cock was hard, begging me to pull over and fuck her, but we were on a timeline and what I had planned couldn't wait. Pushing two fingers inside of her, she started to squeeze, her head fell back, and she moved herself up and down.

"That's it, Princess. Ride my fingers. Make yourself feel good."

"Why are you doing this to me?" She cried.

"Just didn't want to wait all night to see your face when you come. Show me now. Let me see that blissed out look in your eye." Fuck, I should have hired a driver, but I was trying to recreate the first night we went out and that meant I had to drive.

"Chase?" She hissed, then used her hands to move my fingers where she wanted them. As I drove and tried to keep my eye on the road, Becca used me as her own fuck toy and I had never been more sure that I had chosen the right woman.

Without having to say anything else, she started pulsing and losing her breath, coming in my hand. I let her ride out her pleasure and then pulled my fingers to my mouth to taste her. It was torture, but worth it, and I made sure to suck off every last drop until she pulled my hand back onto her leg.

"I needed that," she whispered. "I need you."

"You have me. Forever."

Her smile was bright in the dark car and my heart squeezed in my chest. A few more miles and we were going to be at the happiest place on earth. Our place.

"Disney?" She laughed when she finally saw the signs.

"It's our yearly tradition. We should be getting in right in time for the evening parade."

Just like the year before, she got giddy, and jumped from the car the second we pulled in. Unlike the previous year, though, we were together, holding hands and wrapped in each other's arms as we took our place on the red golf cart.

We were driven to the beginning of the parade route, but instead of getting in line to watch the show, we were taken behind the scenes. Becca looked around in awe, but had no idea what I had planned for her.

When Cinderella approached us, we stood up and let her lead us toward a parade float. It was a horse drawn carriage, lit up, and looked as if it had been created with magic. Becca could barely speak, but she didn't need to. I knew what to do next.

Becca

Chase had made it no secret that he wanted to make Disney our yearly tradition. But I never thought he could out do what he had created when he arranged to have me meet every Disney princess.

Yet there I was, one year later, being escorted into Cinderella's horse-drawn carriage by my very own prince charming. He held my hand and nodded to Cinderella as the door was shut behind us. Then he sat next to me and kissed my cheek.

"You're the princess of the parade tonight."

"This cannot be happening."

"Just wave and smile."

As the horses started trotting, we were pulled from behind the buildings and into the parade and I waved as everyone looked on and waved back. They had no idea who I was, at least I didn't think so, but they were happy for me.

My heart raced as the castle came into view and we made our way down Main Street USA. Chase squeezed my hand, letting me know he was there, but continued to wave to everyone. Somehow, he had topped himself, and I knew I would never forget that moment.

It didn't seem he could ever top the experience of being the princess of the parade, but then, as all the other floats rounded the castle, we veered off and were taken up the ramp. The horses came to a complete stop in front and Chase stood to help me from the carriage.

"What are we doing?" I squealed.

"The princess of the parade is the princess of everything," he explained as if it was a no-brainer. Lifting me by the waist, he set me down on the stoned stage of Cinderella's castle, and we walked to the edge, waving at the crowd.

When he turned, I assumed it was because we had to leave, but the lights changed and an instrumental version of A Dream is a Wish your Heart Makes started playing. Cinderella appeared and handed Chase a microphone and a small box.

Holding my hand, he smirked as realization came over my face. With my free hand, I covered my mouth and started shaking my head. Was he seriously about to do what I thought he was about to do?

"Princess?" He smiled. "You knew I was going to have to bring you back to our place for this, right?"

I didn't even respond, just let the tears flow as he licked his lips with satisfaction.

"I think the night I brought you here last year was the

night I fell in love with you. We didn't kiss, barely held hands, and went our separate ways at the end of the night. But it was the most magical night of my life. Just being in your presence was enough for me. Being near you and making you smile was all that mattered. Fu…" He trailed off, remembering he had an audience and a lot of them were kids. "I mean, dude…" I laughed at his recovery and he cleared his throat. "You were so easy to fall in love with, Cupcake. And I want to spend the rest of my life making you smile the way I did that night. So…."

He went down to one knee and handed Cinderella the microphone. She held it up for him as he opened the box to show me a gorgeous princess-cut diamond. "Will you be my princess forever and marry me?"

All I could do was nod. Even before he finished the question I was nodding, not wasting any time telling him how ready I was to be his wife. He stood quickly and wrapped me into a hug, spinning me around as the crowd roared and the music continued to play louder. When he set me down, he kissed me right as fireworks started going off.

"I don't know how you did it," I cried over the crowd noise. "But this is beyond anything I could have dreamt of."

"There wasn't anything I wouldn't do to make this night the best of your life." He pointed to the crowd, off to the side where a roped off area was. Waving like a maniac was Ali and Cam standing next to my mom and dad. My sisters were also there. Chase's dad was waving as well, standing next to Gary and a few of the players from the Kings. When my eyes went back to Ali and Cam, I saw Kace standing to the side of them, smiling and clapping.

"How did they get here so fast? Kace was at the complex when I left."

"They hustled," Chase laughed. "Then escorted in very quickly while we got settled in the carriage. I knew you wouldn't want me to make a very public proposal and not have them here as well."

Wrapping my arms around his neck, I kissed him as the song came to an end and the crowd cheered one more time. "I love you, Prince Charming."

TWO YEARS LATER

Chase

"Cupcake?" I yelled, freaking out as shit went everywhere.

Literally, shit.

It was on everything.

"What?" She hurried around the corner and immediately started laughing.

"Come get this kid," I gagged.

Scooping our son into her arms, she held him close, as if he wasn't a shit faucet. Don't get me wrong, I loved that baby more than life itself. But I was having to quickly adapt to being shit and puked on in a way I had never imagined.

"My sweet boy," Becca cooed, taking him to the bathroom to clean him up. I followed behind, needing to also clean up and wanting to help her however she needed me.

It had only been a month since we adopted Eric, named after Becca's favorite Disney prince. As ready as I was to be a dad, there was so much I still needed to learn and get used to. Not Becca though. She was made to be a mother. Somehow, all her superpowers were magnified by a thousand percent when Eric was placed in her arms.

If I thought I loved her before, it was nothing compared to

watching her be a mom. I just hoped I lived up to being the dad Eric deserved.

"All clean," Becca said in her sweet motherly voice. I had shed my shirt and she placed Eric in my arms while patting him dry with a towel.

"Grab a diaper before we have another shit show," I urged her, making her laugh.

"Poor daddy." She took Eric from me and placed him on our bed, quickly putting a diaper on and dressing him with something warm for bed.

"Fuck," I whispered, watching her. "You're so fucking sexy when you're in mommy-mode."

She gave me a smile and scrunched her nose up, not quite believing me. In the past month, neither of us had slept much and she had told me she felt like a wicked witch. But Becca would never be anything less than a queen. Our queen.

Eric and I were going to make sure she always knew how beautiful she was.

"Give him to me," I urged, taking the clean baby from her arms. "I'll feed him and rock him. Take a bath, Princess. Relax. Play some music."

"And if he poops again?" She teased.

"I'll handle it. There was no diaper on him that time. He shit while I was cleaning the shit. I panicked."

"You're sexy when you panic," she laughed.

"No the fuck I'm not." I wasn't even going to pretend she meant that.

In a few weeks, Becca was headed back to work and Eric and I were going to be solo and since I insisted that we didn't need a nanny, I was going to have to get over being shit on.

Most days, I worked on charity events and did some TV spots to stay busy. Some days I coached at the high school as an added instructor, other days I helped the Kings with their game. But I wanted to be a stay at home dad for Eric. All of the other stuff could be done around him.

"I love you, Daddy," Becca smiled, then kissed me before walking into the bathroom.

"Love you too, Momma," I winked.

"Come on, big guy," I whispered to Eric. "Let's let mommy rest and I can tell you a story about Uncle Kace going 0-4 tonight at the plate. It's a funny story, you'll love it."

Becca

Settling into a bath, I turned the baby monitor on so I could listen to Chase and Eric. Not because I didn't trust him, but because listening to his stories to Eric were the highlight of my days.

Chase may have panicked when shit went flying, but I had never seen a man so in love with a baby. There had always been a little fear that Chase would resent me for not being able to have a baby for him. But after we got married, he insisted we put our names on an adoption list as soon as possible.

Eric came into our lives faster than we expected, but we jumped at the chance to be his parents. Love at first sight is real. I've lived it, felt it, and know it. My love for him was so strong, there were times I cried thinking about leaving him to go back to work. Guilt ate away at me because I worked for me, not for money.

"So Uncle Kace was playing Arizona tonight. He's been struggling to get hits and he doesn't even know why. I tried telling him he's bringing his head up too soon, but he waves me off and pretends I've never seen him hit before."

Giggling, I shook my head at Chase's story. He really did tell Kace to keep his head down, but Kace didn't wave him off because he didn't believe Chase. Kace waved him off because he's tired too. We were all growing our families and it's exhausting.

"Anyway," Chase continued. "Uncle Cam had a game today too. He did okay, but was sacked twice and I bet his ass hurts. Also, don't tell your mom I told you about Uncle Cam's ass. Or said the word ass."

My eyes were closed, leaning back in the bathtub, but my smile was almost hurting my face.

"Okay enough about those goons. Let's talk about mommy. You have no idea how lucky we are to have her, Buddy. She is the best mommy in the whole world. When you get older, you can help me protect her. We are going to be the best team I ever played on."

My smile had turned to tears as I felt his words in my heart. Reaching up, I turned off the monitor to let them have their talk in private and let my mind wander. The first moment I saw Chase, the way my hand felt when our skin touched, the way he carried me to the office after I got hit with the baseball.

Then I thought about those small touches he gave me when no one was looking, how it felt when he pinned me against the right field wall, and how he did a strip tease with his catcher's gear. Those days were stressful and scary, but I wouldn't change a second of our story. Especially since we survived the lies we told and ended with a happily ever after.

afterword

I started this story 16 years ago when I first tried my hand at writing. After finishing The Games We Play, I decided to resurrect this story and see if I could finish it.

And I did.

Obviously, as the years passed, the original story changed, and I went with the flow. However, keeping the lies straight in my head was kind of hard. Haha.

The one important thing to mention is that some have hated the ending, that Becca and Chase both lost their jobs. They see it as an unhappily ever after, but it was the ultimate WIN for me. I personally know a pro athlete who retired for the same reasons Chase did, giving up the money and the game for a chance at health when it came to his family. So don't be sad. Chase got the ultimate prize! And Becca will make a bigger impact working with future athletes, I promise.

All my love,
Katie

about the author

Katie is a hopeless romantic, a proud mother of two, a devoted wife, and a die-hard baseball fan. She resides in Florida where she loves beach days and boat life.

There is always more to a Katie Rae book than what you think! She loves making us think while also making us swoon. You always think you know, but you have no idea, and that is what makes Katie Rae books so special.

Join the fun in Katie Rae Reader Group and sign up for Katie Rae's Newsletter!

Also, www.katieraebooks.com is now LIVE. Check out extras, events, book information, signed paperbacks, and MORE!

also by katie rae

The GAMES Series (interconnected standalones)

The Games We Play

The Lies We Tell

The Love We Make

The Way We Dance

The Way We Fight

Men of the Military (complete standalones)

Ranger

Raptor

RECON

Rogue

Miami Inferno FC Series (Interconnected Standalones)

Reckless Goals

Scoreless Nights

Twisted Assist

The Boys of Summer Novella

Pretty Boy

Man of the Month Club Novella

Love Bites

Another One Bites the Dust

Silverbell Shore Series (standalone)

Now and Then

Co-Write with Zoey Drake (standalone)

Dirty Monsters

Website Exclusives

The Christmas Playbook (A GAMES Christmas novella)

Manny Christmas (Standalone Christmas novella)

Railbird (A ROGUE short story… free download)